To Aleen

Thanks!

ROADS TO ROME

BY

JT HINE

PREQUEL TO THE *LOCKHART* SERIES

Copyright © 2024 by JT Hine

All rights reserved. No part of this book may be used or reproduced in any manner, including extraction into corpora for machine translation or generative composition database training, without written permission from the author, except for brief quotations in critical articles or reviews. For information, contact: jt@jthine.com.

https://jthine.com

ISBN: 979-8-9865819-5-8 (print)
ISBN: 979-8-9865819-4-1 (eBook)

Book design: ebooklaunch.com

Editor: Kim F. Olson

First edition: December 2024

Dedication

To Clara

Contents

Acknowledgements i
Titles by JT Hine iii
Foreword v
Part I – Sandra 1
  Bullies 1
  Artists 13
  Sandra's first date 25
  Love at first sight 38
  Internship 49
  Sketches 67
  Music and sketches 77
Part II – Joe 91
  Fedhala 92
  Richmond 102
  Inchon 124
  Jason's last wish 133
  Last respects 153
  Grief 161
  Home from the sea, at last 166
  Joe meets the Dama 176
  Lockhart Chapter 1: Bomb 184
Author's Notes 197

Acknowledgements

This collection of short stories unfolded in my two blogs, *Freewheeling Freelancer* and *jthine.com*, over several years. Input from the many readers on my websites has led to the versions of the stories you see here.

The musical selections mentioned come from Daniel Hine, composer, conductor, pianist, violist, and accompanist. It was a no-brainer to make the musically precocious Sandra a violist, too.

Kim Olson at TransConsult edited and proofread the manuscript. Alisha Moore at Ebook Launch designed the cover.

Any mistakes that made it to this version are mine. I would appreciate knowing about them. Email jt@jthine.com.

Titles by JT Hine

Fiction

Lockhart

Enemies

Art to Die for

Emily & Hilda

Rule Number One

Emily Is Hard to Kill

The Marsh

Roads to Rome

The Black Amazon

Aliya

As Our Mothers Made Us

Non-fiction

I Am Worth It!

Are You Bilingual?

Translator Education in the U.S.A.

Translations

Video Games – a Retrospective by Nicolò Mulas Marcello & Alberto Bertolazzi

Combat Aircraft by Riccardo Niccoli

Beyond the Age of Oil by Leonardo Maugeri

Schio: Industrial Archeology by Bernadetta Ricci

Man is Different by Don Zeno (with Emily Adkins)

The Fight against Blindness by Luciano Moretti

The Retirement Correspondence of Thomas Jefferson

Foreword

NANCY, JOE, SANDRA. Three people who star in the novels of the *Lockhart* series. The stories in this collection take place before Joe held the door for Sandra at the Embassy Annex in Rome. Some stories involve their grandparents; others cover the events of their lives that shaped who they are in the novels.

Unlike the novels, these stories were written on deadline. I needed (and still need) a blog post every Saturday afternoon. So, like a preacher who cannot put off writing this week's sermon, I had to write something for my readers. The novel *Lockhart* appeared serially on the blog before I turned it into a book.

This is not historical fiction, which would require more research than a weekly blog would allow. Reference to actual persons or events serves only to put my characters in particular times and places.

Because these appear now in a single book, I have edited the stories to improve the flow and to avoid repeating background that just appeared in the previous tale.

You may skip around if you like. However, I have assembled the stories chronologically. I hope you enjoy them.

I am open to feedback about this project. Email: jt@jthine.com, or use the contact form on my website, https://jthine.com.

Thank you,
JT Hine

Part I – Sandra

Bullies

"LEAVE ME ALONE!" Sandra Billingsley recognized the sobbing voice around the corner. Someone was picking on Karen – *again*, she thought. She slammed her locker door shut and ran around the corner to the hall where the freshman lockers were.

The anger rose in her chest as she spied the Wester brothers each pulling on an arm of her friend. Karen didn't even come up to their shoulders. The tiny Black girl had been bullied mercilessly since the day she arrived from Washington, DC.

For Sandra, the scene triggered rage on so many levels. She had arrived in this Ohio town just two years before, also from Washington. She and Karen had become friends quickly, because Karen's father had also just retired from the Army. Like the Billingsleys before, the Monroe family was starting a new life in the Midwest. As the only 12-year-old in the high school, Sandra had been about the same size as her friend was now. In middle school, she had known the constant terror of large boys and mean girls tormenting her everywhere she turned.

As a freshman, however, Sandra had Marty and Walter. Her eldest brother was a senior and Walter was a junior. No one picked on her after the first week of high school, except her own brothers. Of course, they annoyed her at home on the farm, but she learned to dish it out as good as she got it. Her two younger brothers never tried to wrestle with her after she knocked Marty into the pigs' slop.

By the time Marty had joined the Navy and Walter had left for the Marines, Sandra had begun her growth spurt. Though skinny and gawky, she was taller and stronger than most. A farm was hard work; her parents cut her no slack for being a girl.

Karen did not have anyone. And that really pissed Sandra off.

"You heard her!" She barked. "Karen, drop!" The small girl fell as the two bullies let go to face their furious classmate bearing down on them. Sandra's book bag swung up from behind her butt in an arc that pushed Jerry Wester clear over Karen and into his brother. Sandra reached down even as the inertia of the swinging bag pulled her away from the pair. She caught Karen's wrist and pulled her away from the collapsing heap of adolescent male flesh.

"Get out of the freshman wing, you two. Now!"

Jimmy Wester had a cut on the side of his face, and he was dazed from having hit the floor under the weight of his brother. The two staggered to their feet. Jerry clenched his fists. "What's a nigger to you, Billingsley?" he said.

"A friend—don't even think of it." The book bag was already swinging as Jerry started to move. Another trip to the floor took the rest of the fight out of him. Jimmy helped his brother up, and the two leaned on each other as they staggered to the end of the hall and around the corner.

"Why did you do that?" Karen asked, as Sandra helped her pick up the papers and books that the Westers had pulled from her locker. "I get that all the time, and now you're going to be marked for helping me."

"We Army brats have to stick together, right?" That brought a weak smile to Karen's face. "Besides, the Westers are just bullies. They harassed me, too. People around here know about them."

With the locker stowed and Karen's bag packed, the two friends were barely in time to catch the school bus.

***

"Pass the beans, please, Sandra." Chief Warrant Officer Martin Billingsley, US Army (retired), swung his gaze at his two sons sitting across from Sandra. "What are you two smirking about?"

Their mother paused cutting her steak.

"James, Arnold, answer your father."

Jim looked down at his plate, then at his younger brother, who was staring at a green bean as if willing it to fly, then up to their father.

"Sandy kicked ass today, Dad."

Sandra gasped. Marcia started to speak, but her husband held up his hand. "We'll deal with the language later. What do you mean, son?"

"It's all over the school. You know the Westers in Sandy's class?" Martin nodded. "Well, she beat the sh— heck out of them this afternoon."

Arnie added, "They were picking on Karen Monroe."

"Master Sergeant Monroe's little girl?"

"Yes, sir. She's a freshman."

Martin looked at Sandra. "Is this the pair that got Marty sent to the principal when you were a freshman?"

"Yes, sir. Same ones. It's the third time they've picked on Karen, that I know of. I'd just had enough. Sorry, Dad."

Martin and Marcia exchanged glances. "Pretty thick-headed, aren't they?"

"Yes, sir."

"What about the other two times?"

"Karen didn't want me to report them. She said Negro kids learn to put up with this. The second time, though, I did report them. Nothing happened."

"Does the administration usually ignore bullying?"

"No. Remember those other two guys who tried to pick on me when Marty and Walter were on a band trip? They got suspended for a week."

"You think Karen's suntan makes a difference?"

"I don't know, Dad, but after the second time, I drilled with her, so I could have a clear shot if it happened again."

"Drilled?"

"Just a simple thing. I shout 'drop!' She falls to the floor, which gets her out of the way. I figured it would be the Westers, which meant dealing with two of them."

"So, you practiced fighting?"

"Not really. We practiced her dropping and my swinging the book bag. I always have it with me."

"The principal will be calling us now," said Marcia.

"Who's going to report it, Mom?" said Jim.

"Whoever was there."

Jim and Arnie exchanged glances and giggled again. Their father smiled quickly, then forced a frown at them.

"Who was there, Sandra?"

"Just the four of us, sir. People showed up later, but not before the Westers left."

"So, the only witnesses have to report that they got their heads handed to them by a *girl*," he stretched the word "two years younger than they are?"

"Something like that." Sandra scowled at her brothers. "Oh, stop it, you two. It wasn't funny."

"She's right, boys." Martin looked at his daughter. "What will you do next time, if there are witnesses?"

"The Westers are bullies, Dad. Everyone knows it. The other two times there were people around. All I had to do was confront them. If anyone faces up to them, the other kids come around, and they back down."

Marcia said to her husband, "Now that I've heard this, I'm more concerned about the lack of response from the front office, dear."

"Me too. Sandra, write down the details of what happened when you reported the second bullying: times, dates, who you reported it to, and so forth." He looked back at Marcia. "You're on the faculty, and I'm an angry parent. Let's decide together how to handle this. We should at least talk to Karen's parents."

"I agree. Sandra, can you write that up tonight?"

"Yes, ma'am."

"About the language." Martin scowled at his sons. "You two get KP for the next two days, one for each utterance. Understood?"

"Yes, sir." Having extra turns washing dishes was a light punishment around the Billingsley farm.

***

"Thank you for seeing us, Sergeant."

"Please come in, sir." Zebadiah Monroe stood six-foot-four, all of it muscle. He took their coats, and introduced his wife, Samara. Mrs. Monroe was a tall woman, easily five-eleven, slender, with angular features.

"We're both retired. Would you call me Martin?"

"Zeb, then."

They settled in the living room, where coffee was waiting, with some small cakes. Martin and Marcia both took in the shadow box with Zeb's ribbons and medals: Combat infantry, paratrooper, and Special Forces. Marcia's eyes were drawn immediately to the pictures on the walls.

"These are fantastic – and familiar. Who is the artist?"

Zeb laughed and patted his wife's shoulder, "I told you that you couldn't hide out here in the Midwest, dear."

Marcia gasped, "Samara. Of course! Samara Majib. You were teaching at the George Washington University. We saw your exhibition at the Corcoran a few years back."

Samara smiled and looked down modestly. "Guilty as charged."

Martin cleared his throat softly. "I think you two need to meet for shop talk. It will be over my head, for sure."

"Me too," said Zeb, shifting to face Martin more directly. "On the phone, you sounded very concerned."

Marcia answered. "We are. You know I'm Karen's art teacher, don't you?"

"Yes, is this a parent-teacher conference?"

"Goodness, no, though I understand Karen's work now, meeting you, Samara. It's about our daughter

Sandra, who has befriended Karen since school started. Has Karen talked to you about the bullying at school?"

"A little. She has been dealing with bullies all her school years," said Samara. "And she has talked with some enthusiasm about Sandra. Sandy, she calls her. As far as I can tell, your daughter is her hero."

"They are friends," said Martin, "and Sandra does not suffer bullies lightly. Her older brothers protected her when she was a freshman, until she grew a little and could handle herself."

"And Karen?"

"Karen is even smaller than Sandra was in middle school and freshman year, and she was bothered by some of the same bullies when we came here. Things came to a head last week."

"The Wester boys?"

"She basically trashed them. No witnesses, so officially, no one will probably hear about it."

Zeb smiled at that. "A senior and a junior beat up by a girl?"

"And one who's two years younger."

Martin said, "We wanted to talk to you about the earlier bullying before we go to the administration. After all, Karen is the victim here."

Martin and Marcia outlined what they had learned from Sandra about the lack of response to the earlier incidents. Zeb and Samara admitted that Karen had told them about a half-dozen cases of insults and shoving when Sandra was not around.

"It seems that Assistant Principal Engels is the key to this," said Marcia. "He received Sandra's complaint, and he is responsible for discipline."

"You mean he doesn't discipline?" Samara asked.

Martin and Marcia looked at each other. "That's why we're here. We think there's racial bias involved, because he did suspend some students who bullied Sandra when she was a freshman."

"What do you propose?"

"Not sure, but we know we shouldn't take action without discussing it with you. We're almost as new here as you are, so we don't know if the problem is deeper than one administrator. After all, the Wester boys didn't get their language or behavior from Mr. Engels. That's their parents and their friends."

"Makes me miss the Army even more," said Zeb. "At least we felt like we had some recourse against the bigots when they acted out."

"I understand that."

"Then there's your situation, Marcia," said Samara. "Isn't this Assistant Principal your superior?"

"Yes, although the District Fine Arts Coordinator looks out for his special teachers. Still, it won't be pretty if we go public with this."

"We're not looking for a solution tonight," said Martin, "but any ideas would be appreciated, and we don't want to move on this unless you're on board with it."

"I'm glad you're not trying to rush this. Our daughter may get ahead of us if we let her."

"Meaning?"

"Karen may do what Sandy did. Start growing in time not to need help."

"Oh, of course. Looking at the two of you, that will be impressive."

"Yes. Meanwhile, maybe I could teach her some moves. She'll need them if she turns out half as beautiful as her mother." He smiled at Samara.

"I feel better, Zeb," said Martin. "We came here as an angry father and a vulnerable teacher. I'll hold off until we talk some more. I have all the details on the report that the Assistant Principal ignored. I'll make a copy for you."

"Thanks. I have an idea about it." He walked over to the desk, where he retrieved a folder. "These are my notes from what Karen told us. I'll add your material. If this follows the pattern I think it will, I may just pass a suggestion to a friend." He smiled. "Everyone has a boss, even the Assistant Principal."

Martin and Marcia stood. She said, "Are you free after school hours, Samara?"

"Yes. Karen can babysit Zeb here." They chuckled.

"Shall we hold a parent-teacher conference in that new espresso bar next to the courthouse?"

"Excellent. Four-thirty tomorrow?"

"I'm looking forward to it very much."

***

Sandra and Karen sat on the little pier that Sandra and her brothers had built. They had taken off their shoes and were swinging their feet in the duck pond. Saturday of Indian summer was almost as hot as September had been. The Monroes had come over for lunch. The grown-ups were chatting on the back porch. Jim and Arnie had taken their bikes to the junior high school for orchestra rehearsal.

"That's a new dress, Karen. Nice."

"Thanks. Mom says she'll need to start sewing, because I'm starting to grow."

"Last year, I was about your size. I grew all this much since then."

"I wish I were taller. Then the Westers wouldn't bother me so much."

"You will be. Look at your parents. I bet you'll be taller than I am."

"Hard to believe."

"Well, trust me. It happens. Neither of my older brothers wore out a pair of jeans or shoes, and Jim and Arnie are wearing them now."

"One advantage of siblings."

"And you have tits," said Sandra. She ran her hands over her own flat chest.

"I wish I didn't. Boys are starting to notice, and it bugs me."

"Have you had your period?"

"Yeah. Started last month. Not much yet. Another thing I don't look forward to. You?"

"Not yet. My mother says the women in her family tend to start late. I hope I don't start in the middle of gym class or something embarrassing like that."

"My mother made me carry a pad in my purse starting last year. She said she could tell I was going to need it."

"Well, maybe I can get out of high school first. I hear that college kids don't care about stuff like periods and hair."

Sandra reached over and picked up a flat stone. She skipped it across the pond.

"How'd you do that?"

"You never skipped stones?"

"Probably would have gotten arrested trying that in the pool on the National Mall."

Sandra laughed and stood. She selected some flat, smooth stones. They skipped stones until Karen could almost reach across the pond. Most of Sandra's stones were lying on the far shore.

"Want some orange juice? I'm thirsty."

"Sure."

On the way to the house, Sandra asked, "Any more trouble with the Westers or any of the others?"

"Not since I talked to Dad after our last run-in."

"You told your father?"

"Oh, yes, then I had to tell him how awesome you were and please don't go teach the Westers a lesson."

"But I just swung my book bag at them."

"That's not the point. When he calmed down, he said he would teach me self-defense. He even apologized for not noticing sooner that he should have been doing that."

"Like hand-to-hand?"

"Of course. He was a Green Beret, you know. He could kill you with one hand."

"Scary."

"Yeah, but he told me it's mostly attitude and knowing how to stay out of a fight when possible. He said he'd teach me that, too, and how to pick my fights so I don't take the rap for them."

"My brother Marty could have used that lesson."

"You told me about that one. I think your dad and mine have something cooked up."

"What are they doing?"

"I don't know, but after your folks came to our house last week, Doctor Mitford came."

"I've never heard of the principal visiting anyone's home."

"Me, neither. Anyway, they went into Dad's study for an hour, then he left."

***

Sandra caught up with Karen getting on the school bus.

"Karen, did you hear about Mr. Engels?"

"I was supposed to see him today, but he wasn't in. Mrs. Spivey told me to go back to class."

"He's not coming back."

"Why?"

"Apparently, last week, Doctor Mitford asked Mrs. Spivey for the files on student complaints for the last three years. Mr. Engels was breaking all kinds of rules handling them. I don't know the details, but the faculty had a briefing after lunch today. Mom told me that Mrs. Schmidt will be Acting Assistant Principal until they can hire a new one."

"Wow! Does this have anything to do with the Westers?"

"I don't know, but Mom said we should feel free to report any bullying. Not just them. Apparently, Mr. Engels wasn't investigating complaints or documenting outcomes. Mrs. Schmidt won't be like that; you can count on it."

Artists

SANDRA AND KAREN finished their orange juice and looked out the window to the back porch. Their parents were deeply engrossed in conversation. Sandra could tell that the fathers were swapping war stories about their Army days, but she was surprised that the mothers were discussing an art exhibit at the Columbus Museum.

"Want to see my room?" Sandra asked her friend.

"Sure!" They rinsed out their glasses and went upstairs.

"Oh, Sandy, you *paint!*" Karen walked up to the pictures hanging in Sandra's room. "These are lovely."

"Thank you. Most of them were homework. My mother *is* the art teacher, you know. I call them her commissions. Sounds fancier."

"Your detail is like a Renaissance master."

"Oh, c'mon, Karen. I'm just painting what's there. But thanks."

"Who did the pictures in the living room and the stairway?"

"Everything else is by my mother."

"My mother paints, too. Pictures make a house a home, I think."

"Yeah."

"You play viola, too?" Karen admired the instrument sitting on its case on the dresser. "I know you're in orchestra at school."

"Yeah. Dad's the musician. None of us escaped piano and voice, and he made each of us learn another instrument."

"Do you play together?"

"Sure. Although we play mostly quartets now, with Marty and Walter gone, and Arnie is still learning."

"I think that's wonderful."

Sandra smiled. "You said your mother paints. What about you?"

"Nothing like Mom, but she makes me work at it."

"Could I come over and see them sometime?"

"Anytime. I'm sure my folks will be inviting you over. They're getting along famously down there." A loud burst of laughter floated into the open window. The girls chuckled. "But you can come anytime you like. It's not like we live on the other side of town."

Sandra's father knocked on the door. He was smiling when Sandra opened it.

"You two better get out there. It's turning into a parent-teacher conference. And you, young lady, are the subject." He nodded at Karen.

Karen gasped, and the two friends walked quickly down to the porch. No one was there.

"Over here, girls."

Marcia Billingsley and Samara Monroe were in the living room, standing in front of a landscape that Sandra's mother had painted.

"You probably don't remember this lady from Washington, do you, Sandra?"

"Uh, no, but there is something familiar about her."

"Just what I said. And I found out why Karen here is so good in art class. You were eleven when we went to the exhibit at the Corcoran, but you were rather taken by some of the pictures there. Ring a bell?"

"Samara Majib. Deserts and highlands. Village life and African cities." Sandra's jaw dropped. "You, ma'am?"

"Guilty as charged. And I am flattered that you remember."

"Oh, I wanted so much to be able to paint like that." She turned to her friend. "Karen, I never knew!"

Karen smiled and looked down. "She's just Mom around the house, you know."

"Ms. Majib – I mean Mrs. Monroe, what happened to the portrait of the young woman with Mount Kilimanjaro behind her shoulder? It was my favorite."

Samara arched her eyebrows and smiled at the Billingsleys. "You have a prodigious memory, Sandra. I still have it. It is my favorite, too, though we could have stopped saving for Karen's college if I sold it."

"Can I come see it? I already told Karen I want to come see her paintings."

"Of course. Anytime."

Karen had been watching with a nervous expression. "What's this about a parent-teacher conference, Mom?"

"That's my fault," said Martin. "Sorry, Karen. It was a joke. These two will probably be having art conferences every week at that new coffee shop near the courthouse."

"Oh, okay." Karen said, with a sigh of relief.

"Sandra," said Samara, "if you remember *Bride of the Chief* after so long, can you tell me why you like it so much?"

"Yes, ma'am." Sandra crossed the living room to the bookshelf. She selected an art history textbook and opened it to the color plates in the middle. The corners were worn from frequent fingering, and the book fell open to *Young Woman with a Unicorn,* by Raffaello. She held the book up to give it to Karen's mother.

Samara looked at the picture in stunned silence, then lifted her eyes to Sandra's mother. "Well done, Marcia, very well done."

"The children are often the teachers around here, right, Martin?"

"Absolutely."

"Sandra, I have this same book at home. Your mother and I probably both used it in college." Marcia nodded. "Have you seen *Dama con Liocorno?*"

"No. It's in Rome. I'll get there some day." She looked sternly at her parents.

"No doubt. Meanwhile, when you come to see Karen, could we spend some time in front of the *Bride* with this photo? I would love to hear more."

"Sure. That would be cool."

***

Winter came with a vengeance on Monday morning. By Thanksgiving, Ohio had been buried twice in record snowfalls. Sandra found herself looking at a second semester with no required courses for her high school diploma. She decided to apply for early admission to college.

Her parents could hardly argue with her. Now that she was taller than most of the girls in her class, no one seemed to notice her age. She had met the academic requirements, with a 4.0 grade point average. The experts liked to write about the importance of social interactions, but Sandra exuded self-confidence. After handling bullies, mean girls and the occasional bigot who resented her friendship with Karen, she would come out of high school better prepared than her classmates would the following year.

"But where?"

"That's easy, Mom." Sandra said as she swept the snow off the front porch. Marcia shook out the doormats. "George Washington."

"We don't have any family in DC, dear."

"Why do I need family? The idea is to go *away* to college, isn't it?"

"Let's talk to your father about this."

"Already did. He's all for it. But if you want to have a threesome, I'm OK with it. Guidance won't let me apply without your approval."

"GW is a hard school to get into. And it's private." Sandra knew that her mother meant "expensive," but she had also researched the student aid and scholarship opportunities.

"If I don't make it. I'll have all next year to work on a re-attack or change plans."

"Let's talk to your father. I need it; apparently your mind is made up."

Martin shouted from the pig enclosure near the barn. "Honey, could you spare Sandra from the light duty? Arnie will never get all that hay from the loft to the stalls by sundown."

"Okay, dear." She turned to her daughter. "Don't forget your muck boots. Go."

"Yes, ma'am." She ran in and changed her footwear. "Coming, Dad!"

***

The week before the Christmas break, the senior Civics class boarded a bus for a field trip to the courthouse. This was Sandra's last required course. With the holidays coming, attention spans were shorter than the days, and both teachers and students were glad for an outing. Sandra toted her heavy book bag; the older kids gave her space, knowing the blonde junior to be armed and dangerous.

They filed in as quietly as twenty teenagers can, and sat in the first two rows of the public section, just in front of the journalists. Sandra sat on the end near the windows, so the light came over her shoulder. She took out her sketchbook and pencil case.

The case before the court involved a murder stemming from an argument in a bar in early September. The class had studied the jury system, the burden of proof, and the process of jury selection. While waiting for things to start, most of the students were reading or trying not to doze off. The room was full, because murder is always more interesting than a property dispute or tax evasion. The bodies added to the heat from the old radiators, putting some of the public to sleep.

Sandra was wide-eyed, taking in the neo-classical architectural details of the room and the expressions of the different groups of people. Her pencils flew over her sketchbook as she drew the room from different points of view. An artist can put herself in the front of the room and look back; a photographer can't.

When the trial began, she focused on the people up front. She was particularly taken by the different reactions of the potential jurors during the *voir dire*. Sometimes she would close her eyes to picture a disappointed juror being rejected – or accepted, and sketch as quickly as she could before the next event.

At four-thirty, the judge called a short recess, "to allow the school children to exit."

Sandra looked in alarm at her teacher approached her.

"Mrs. Schmidt, may I stay? I can walk home. I would really like to see at least the prosecution's presentation." The teacher's face darkened like a bureaucrat about to miss her lunch break. Then the expression cleared.

"Okay, Miss Billingsley, but use the recess to call your parents. They need to know where you are."

"Thank you, ma'am." She shouldered her book bag and ran to the pay phones in the hall, almost knocking over a journalist in the aisle.

***

When court adjourned for the day, the sun had long gone down. Sandra stood and turned around to put her sketchbook and pencils away. A journalist was standing there. Just under six feet tall, sandy hair, clean-shaven with his hat crushed under his arm and his notepad in his right hand.

As he stuffed the pad in his coat pocket, he asked, "Miss Billingsley, isn't it?"

"Yes?"

"I'm Randy Schmidt—no relation to Doris, your teacher." He smiled. "I'm with the *Messenger*, and our sketch artist called in sick today. I couldn't help seeing you drawing. May I see?"

Sandra pulled out her sketchbook. "They're just sketches, I have to fill in the details from my notes and memory later."

"I know how it works; I've watched Mirella. These are amazing." He reached into his pocket. "Here's my card. I am sure that the editor would like to run some of your sketches with the story. May we call you tonight?"

"Sure. We're in the phone book."

"Thanks." He shook her hand. "Can I give you a lift?"

"No, thanks. That's my dad at the back of the room. I'll be fine."

"Good. See you tomorrow?"

"Only if I can get off my afternoon classes. Your editor may have to call a school official in the morning."

"He can do that. Later, then."

The editor did call about nine and came to the house with a freelance contract. They would pay twenty dollars for each picture they used. They would return the originals unharmed. He would call the school in the morning. Sandra would make her way to and from the courthouse. Martin gave permission for Randy Schmidt to drive her home if necessary. He knew Randy from church.

The next morning, Mrs. Schmidt found Sandra at lunch and told her that the court would convene at one p.m. each day, and she had permission to attend. It would be counted as a special term paper for Civics.

"Congratulations, Miss Billingsley. I've never had special work in Civics before. Would you mind giving a talk to the class when the case is over?"

"Not at all, ma'am. Thank you."

Karen had seen the exchange. "Sandy, that's so cool! You're a freelance court artist now."

"Here, Karen. I can't finish this." She gave her cherry pie to her friend and rushed to her locker. She had ridden her bicycle to school, hoping that this would happen. Lucky for her, they lived off Highway 38, which the Department of Transportation kept cleared all winter.

The case ran for the rest of the week. The jurors filed out on Saturday morning, having found the accused guilty of a lesser charge.

The letters to the editor that week were filled with praise for the illustrations. Sandra had captured the emotions of the parties, they wrote, in a way that made the proceedings come alive. Many wrote that they had never appreciated the personal stakes for the people in the room until they saw Sandra's sketches.

School let out, and the Billingsley family could relax for a couple of weeks. Only the cow and the goats needed to be milked at dawn; otherwise, they could stretch out their chores.

The church asked them to provide the string quartet for the Christmas Vigil service, and they extended their rehearsals at home with an hour or so of each of their favorites. Some of those were even Christmas pieces.

On December 23, the editor called. He asked to come by the house again.

When they were settled in the living room with coffee, the editor said, "I have some bad news and some good news – at least I hope it's good."

"I hope the paper isn't closing," said Marcia.

"No. In fact, advertising and subscriptions increased after the court case coverage. Thank you, Sandra."

Sandra did not know what to say besides, "You're welcome. Could we have the bad news first?"

"Mirella, the artist you replaced in the courtroom, is quite ill. She is not only sick; she's pregnant, and it will be a dangerous pregnancy. Her husband is taking her to New Mexico to be with her extended family and in somewhat warmer weather.

"The good news, for the paper at least, is that it's not permanent, and there is an excellent artist in town." He looked at Marcia. "Two, actually."

"I don't do on-the-spot sketches like that," said Sandra's mother. "She has amazed me as much as everyone else."

"Sandra, we'd like to hire you as our court artist for the rest of Mirella's pregnancy. She is due in June, so we are talking about the rest of the school year, and maybe some of the summer."

"What about my classes?"

"We thought of that. I've already had a meeting with the principal and your curriculum committee. I didn't realize that you have already finished the coursework for your diploma."

"Yes, sir, but I have to attend school for another semester."

"We found a solution to that. The school is willing to schedule all your classes in the morning and release you in the afternoon."

"This sounds like a proper job, sir. You'll be paying me?"

"Yes. The same twenty dollars for each sketch we use, and the same wage we pay reporters: five dollars an hour whenever you are on the clock."

"When would I be on the clock?"

"In court or on the premises of the newspaper, or—this would be unusual—if you go out on another assignment."

"Taxes?"

The editor looked at her parents and smiled.

"Your choice. As a freelancer, you'd pay all your own taxes; we would not withhold. Some reporters want to be part-time employees, so we withhold Social Security and income tax for them. Simplifies their tax reporting at the end of the year."

"I get Social Security credit if you make me a part-timer, don't I?"

"Someone was awake in Civics class, I see. Yes, you would get Social Security credit for two quarters."

"I'll take term employment if you don't mind. It will be cool to have my Social Security record starting already. What about when there are no court cases?"

"You're free to do whatever you need to, as long as we can call you in if there is something urgent to cover. Those are rare here."

"Anything else I should know?"

'Yes. Filling the hours of school required by the state. I reached out to my college roommate, who is on the Journalism faculty at Ohio State University. You can register for their extension school and earn three credits for JRN505. It's an independent study elective focusing on images. All you have to do is submit the portfolio of what you sketch, which we will have at the newspaper. My recommendation as your advisor is all they need."

"Cool, I'm already in college!"

"I thought you'd like that." He looked to Martin and Marcia. "Is all of this okay with you? We'll need your signatures on the employment contract and other paperwork. And she'll need a Social Security card."

Martin smiled at his daughter. "She has that, but I guess we'd better dig it out of her baby papers and give it to her."

Sandra's First Date

SANDRA LOCKED HER BICYCLE to the parking sign outside the *Madison Messenger* building. She caught her breath standing in the sunshine on the sidewalk. It had been a warm day for early April, and she had sweated through her clothes.

To the south, she could see dark, rolling clouds gathering against the intense blue of the rest of the sky. The wind had been coming from that direction, so she expected that she might have a wet slog home.

Even here in the city, the air smelled of new plants: trees, crops, grass. Planting had only started this month, but spring was impatient to burst forth.

"Hi, Sandra. You're early." Randy Schmidt, the reporter whom she shadowed when she was not drawing in court, stood at the copy machine. He picked up his copies and walked with her to their cubicle.

"I got held up after my last class, so I skipped lunch to get here."

"Real reporters eat at their desks." He pulled a brown paper bag from a drawer. "We can 'do lunch'."

"Does this count as a lunch date?"

Randy laughed. "Think your dad will mind?"

"I wouldn't know. I've never been on a date."

Sandra settled into her side of the cubicle and extracted her lunch from the messenger bag she carried when she rode. They both ate silently for the first few bites.

"No court today," she said. "Do you have an assignment this afternoon?"

"Not yet, so I'll go to the nursing home with the photographer. Do you want me to make up something for you?"

Randy was responsible for keeping her busy when there was no work for her as a sketch artist. So far, she had learned how to replace the corona wire in the photocopier, clean and repair the fax machine, maintain the typewriters, and sharpen several hundred pencils. She also wrote draft copy for the reporters when there was too much material for them to write it all by deadline.

"No, thanks. I'd like to finish writing up the text to go with the pictures from the county jail last week. Then all I'll need is to visit the probation office."

"Want me to set that up?"

"I called them last week, and we agreed to visit this week. Would Friday be good?"

"Friday afternoon. I'll call them to confirm it and get someone to cover for me if any calls come in while we're out." He put the waxed paper from his sandwich in the wastebasket and took out an apple. "You know, Sandra, this special spread on criminal justice is going to be a big hit."

"I'm just glad Mr. Manning likes it. It's been fun and exciting to put it together."

Sandra had been working afternoons at the *Messenger* since Christmas. The regular sketch artist was in New

Mexico, convalescing and pregnant. She was expected back in June, after Sandra graduated from high school. For Sandra's last semester, Joseph Manning, the editor, had arranged for her to enroll in JRN505 at Ohio State University, which made the hours at the newspaper count for school credit. The school gave her afternoons off because she had met the course requirements for graduation.

As a sketch artist, Sandra accompanied Randy to court whenever it was in session. She also went with him to the police station, on patrol with the county sheriff, to arraignments, grand jury meetings, and the hospital when injuries were involved.

The reaction to her sketches had been enthusiastic, and readership of the *Messenger* increased every time an issue came out with her artwork.

Last month, she had pitched the idea of a special issue on the criminal justice system, from arrest through the police and court systems, to prison, and back out through the parole system. The editor approved it and asked Sandra to work on it whenever she was not on call with Randy.

Their lunches finished, Randy left to interview a nursing home resident, taking the staff photographer with him. Sandra rolled a sheet of paper into her typewriter and started to write.

***

When Sandra pushed out the door at five o'clock, the sky was darkening rapidly, though sunset was a couple of hours away. A stiff breeze from the south pushed debris up Main Street and across High Street. *With this breeze,*

I should get home before the rain hits, she thought. She mounted her bicycle and leaned into the crosswind for the two blocks on High Street before turning north on Highway 38.

The first heavy drops pelted her when she still was two miles from home. In seconds, that turned into something like a giant bucket being emptied on her head.

In no time, water was running inside her jacket and down her skin. She might as well be swimming. *At least it's not cold.*

She kept riding as fast as she could, pushed by the half-gale blowing her along.

She passed a large billboard for Skoal chewing tobacco. With her head down and concentrating on getting home, she did not recognize the frisson of her hair standing up.

A blinding white light surrounded her. Her scream was lost in the sound around her.

The light subsided quickly. The sound (*was that an explosion?*) receded, replaced by a loud ringing in her ears. *Where am I? What am I?*

The questions refocused her mind and caused her to take stock of her situation. She felt and saw the gravel in front of her head and recognized the edge of the asphalt. Her right knee and the right side of her face burned.

Testing her joints, she found that she could move, and she got up. She had a hole in her right trouser leg and road rash. Her left wrist and hand had some abrasions, but her watch had taken most of the blow. The watch band was a bracelet now.

Her bicycle lay in the ditch about ten feet up the road. Only half the billboard was still attached to its upright, blowing in the wind like a flag. The other half was in pieces, most of them black and some still smoking, strewn downwind for about fifty feet.

Shaking herself off, Sandra walked to her bicycle. She remembered the oft-repeated warning not to ride in a thunderstorm and swore at herself. She would allow herself to feel grateful for her close escape later.

Still distracted, she almost swung back into the saddle. She noticed that her front tire was flat. Not just flat but destroyed. A large staple or nail, probably from the billboard, ran through the tire and the inner tube. She could smell the rubber that had melted around the nail.

Visibility was down to less than a couple of car lengths. *I hope everyone slows down.* She began pushing her bicycle towards home, hoping to make it to the shelter of the school bus stop near their driveway. She had no idea how long she had been unconscious, but it occurred to her that it was closer to sunset than it should have been. She turned on her taillight, which seemed almost useless in the downpour.

A full-sized pickup truck passed her, splashing her as it went by. She muttered one of the oaths her father used when he smashed his thumb, laughing at herself as she did it.

The pickup stopped almost out of sight. Instead of backing up, the driver jumped out and ran toward her.

"Sandra! What the hell are you doing out here?" She recognized the broad shoulders and messy brown hair, now slicked down around his head. Bill Southern was a senior and the editor of the high school newspaper. Sandra had been one of his writers until the *Messenger* job took her away from school every afternoon.

"Hi, Bill. You're getting soaked."

"Never mind me, what happened to you?"

"I think it was a lightning strike. Slashed my front tire." She pointed to the destroyed billboard.

"Jeez, that wheel stinks. Let's get your bike in the back." He picked up the bike easily and carried it to the back of the truck.

The rain stopped as they pulled onto the road.

Ten minutes later, Bill pulled up outside the Billingsley farmhouse. Marcia and Martin both came out. Marcia ran to her daughter, while Martin shook hands and thanked Bill for bringing Sandra home. They got the bike out of the truck, and Bill drove off.

Inside, finally safe, Sandra began shaking.

***

Bill caught up with Sandra as the students filed out of Spanish class.

"Hey, Sandra, got a minute?"

"What's up?"

"I never see you at lunch anymore."

"I pack it now and eat it at the *Messenger*."

"Makes sense. I envy you, working at a real newspaper."

Sandra shrugged. "Aren't you planning to major in journalism at OSU?"

"Yeah."

They arrived at Sandra's locker. She began organizing her messenger bag. Bill leaned on the next locker.

"You're a junior. Got a date for the prom?"

"No. I hadn't even thought of it, and no one has asked. I *am* younger than the others, you know."

"That doesn't bother me. Would you like to go? We're both going to college next year, so it's our last chance."

"Sure. I figured that was something I would miss. Let me clear it with my parents, but I can't see why they'd say no."

"Great. I can't afford a limo, but maybe I can get Dad to lend me the car. The truck is past being able to clean."

"If we take the truck, we can wear overalls instead of a tux and a gown, eh?"

He laughed. "Let me know tomorrow. Thanks."

"Thank *you*, Bill." She smiled as he skipped down the hall.

***

Parental permission was the easy part. Bill confirmed that his father would let him drive the family car, if he cleaned it and detailed it.

Her mother asked the harder question, "What will you wear?" Neither Marcia nor her daughter followed fashion, so the Billingsley family lacked those kinds of magazines. Sandra picked up what she could at the Rexall drugstore, and she pored over them with her mother for several nights. They both sketched ideas from what they saw.

The following Saturday, Marcia drove Sandra to Columbus. They came back with a pattern and fabric. The dress would follow Sandra's figure nicely, with room below the waist for dancing, running, and other activities. With no straps, it drew attention to her blond hair and her strong shoulders, giving the observer something to notice instead of her relatively flat chest.

Most important, Marcia guessed that it would be the easiest pattern to follow. As Sandra worked the sewing machine, she was grateful for her mother's insight.

Unspoken was why an eighteen-year-old senior would invite a fifteen-year-old to the prom. But Bill and Sandra had known each other since Sandra arrived in seventh grade, and they had worked on the school papers and yearbooks all that time. Martin and Marcia knew that he was a shy boy, and that he had been bullied in middle school. He had not taken anyone to the prom the year before.

***

Bill stood at the foot of the stairs and gawked. Sandra barely caught her own jaw. She had never seen him in anything but jeans, his hair almost never combed. The new tuxedo fit him well. She was surprised to feel a stirring at his appearance that she had never felt before.

"My god, Sandra, you look fabulous!"

Sandra patted her hair to make sure it was still there.

"Mom gets the credit for the hairdo. I've never put it up."

"I mean, the whole package. That dress makes you look – well, great!"

"Thanks, Bill. You look good yourself."

Martin and Marcia appeared on the porch. They could see that the two young people wanted to get on with their adventure.

"What time do you want me to bring her back, sir?"

"I don't expect you to go clubbing in Columbus," said Martin, "so bring her back when she tires of you. She knows we have to sing in church tomorrow."

"My dad wants the car back by one, so it will be earlier than that."

"Fine. Have fun, you two."

***

Sandra felt exposed. She blushed as Bill took her arm and led her down the hallway to the gymnasium. It had never occurred to her to go to the school dances before this year. She was delighted to discover how much she liked dancing, and to find that she could do it without tripping or stepping on her partner.

Still, this was her first date, and she had never walked on a boy's arm before. The many stares they got may have been for Bill – he *was* easy on the eyes – but she also met a lot of surprised gazes.

"It's a stage, dear," her mother had said. "Just like our concerts. Head up and let the confidence flow." Martin, a retired Army musician, had made sure all his children learned an instrument in addition to voice. They performed regularly throughout Madison County and sometimes in Columbus or Springfield.

Sandra smiled and returned the greetings of those friends who snapped out of it soon enough to say something.

As they danced, Sandra was glad that her gown was light weight and sleeveless. The old gym could have used air conditioning tonight. She danced mostly with Bill, but also with her friends in the high school orchestra and the other boys on the school paper.

She was surprised to see Master Sergeant Monroe and his wife Samara on the sidelines among the chaperones.

She introduced Bill, then took him to meet her friend Karen, a freshman.

Karen was in awe of the tall, handsome senior, but also delighted to be at a dance with her friend Sandra. Sandra was pleased to see that the Wester brothers, who had bullied Karen in the fall, did not show up.

Most especially, she enjoyed the feeling of dancing close with Bill. Not at all the same as dancing with her father, or older brothers (who were long gone from home). From what she could tell, Bill liked it, too.

She wasn't ready to stop when the orchestra leader announced the last dance.

***

"It's only eleven," Bill said as they walked to the car. "Want to go somewhere else?"

"I didn't get a chance to visit the food table. I could split a pizza if you like."

"Mamma Leone's?"

"Sure."

She tugged a little on his arm and smiled. The pizzeria was across the street from the *Messenger* building.

On the sidewalk outside the restaurant, Sandra heard a familiar voice behind them.

"Cradle-robbing tonight, Southern?" Jerry Wester. As he approached, Sandra could smell the beer. They turned toward the door, so they could see him. His brother Jimmy was with him.

"From what I hear, you two need to mind your business," said Bill.

"Little girl ain't toting her deadly book bag tonight."

"That's not my only weapon, Jerry," said Sandra. "Back off. Now."

"I don't like your tone, bitch. Do you, Jimmy?"

"No." They both rushed at Bill and Sandra.

Jerry was on Sandra's side. He ran full tilt into her raised knee and doubled over, as she straightened her leg, and her right heel nailed his foot to the pavement. He flew forward and fell face down.

Jimmy met a solid right punch to his solar plexus and also fell as Bill brought his left fist down on the side of Jimmy's head.

For a moment, Sandra and Bill looked at each other in surprise.

The two Westers scrambled to get up. Bill held the door for Sandra, and they slipped into the pizzeria. He leaned on the door long enough for Jerry to slam into it and reconsider taking the fight into the establishment.

"That was exciting," Bill said, as they pulled slices of the medium four-seasons pizza to their plates. "You didn't scream or anything. You were awesome."

"I've been running into them ever since we moved here. If there had been time to think, I would have been scared."

"I heard about your book bag."

"Yeah. Karen and I worked on that until they stopped picking on her."

"Well, I feel safer with you around, too. Want to go out again, maybe with more casual clothing?"

"What do you have in mind?"

"A movie? *Spartacus* and *El Cid* are both in town."

"So is *La Dolce Vita*," she said with a mischievous smile. "I've always wanted to go to Rome."

"I'd like that, too, but they won't let us in."

"Kirk Douglas and Charlton Heston are fine with me. You pick one. I'll ask my folks about next Saturday. Okay?"

"Okay."

Bill pulled in front of the Billingsley house at midnight. He stayed for a while to chat and got permission to take Sandra to the movies the following weekend.

With the gown hanging and her hair down, she went to the kitchen for a glass of water. Her parents had already gone to bed.

She lay in her bed and stared at the ceiling. She did not want to fall asleep. Instead, she wanted to revel in the Cinderella feeling of the evening. Her body had other ideas after all the exercise, and soon she was fast asleep, dreaming of adventures in Rome with men who moved like Bill but whose faces she could not see.

***

Sandra's last semester in high school passed in a blur.

Between cases at the courthouse, Sandra followed Randy on his city beat, when he did not have a photographer. The editor loved the special feature Sandra had pitched back in March, and the newspaper ran three extra printings, all of which sold out. They prepared a special-order edition of the spread, which continued to sell long after Sandra left town, notably to high school teachers throughout the state. In addition to her chores on the farm, she played with the school orchestra and made time to ride her bicycle with Karen out to Choctaw Lake.

To her mother's surprise, the George Washington University offered her a full scholarship from a little-used endowment in the Department of Fine Arts. Samara, the editor, and even the judge wrote recommendation letters. Her portfolio of sketches and the painted "commissions" for her mother the art teacher impressed the faculty. One of Samara's friends on the committee called her to say that the criminal justice spread put Sandra over the top. "Few artists can also write that well. She'll be an asset to the school."

Arturo and Maria Menendez, lead bassoonist and clarinetist in the National Symphony Orchestra, offered to have Sandra stay with them. The Menendezes were close family friends and lived in Foggy Bottom near the University. Sandra and Selena had been best friends until Martin's retirement. That eased Marcia's worries in part.

Working around the newspaper, Sandra not only learned to write copy on deadline, compose articles and type very fast, but also to operate the new machines that were becoming ubiquitous in newsrooms everywhere: fax machines, telexes, and photocopiers. Her attention to detail caused her articles to sparkle. Little did she know how those skills would shape her future two years after the family piled into the station wagon to drive her to Washington, DC for her college adventures.

Love at First Sight

SANDRA BILLINGSLEY pushed the door to the classroom and stood, staring in awe.

"Hey, why'd you stop?" A heavyset boy crashed into her back.

"Sorry." She jumped to the side to let him pass.

The lecture hall was laid out as an amphitheater, with at least thirty rows of seats. Down at the bottom, where she was standing, a table with a Vu-graph overhead projector sat next to a lectern. A graduate assistant was adjusting the projection of a test transparency on the screen above the shallow stage behind the table and lectern.

She climbed up the inside wall to a row with free seats. She wasn't late, but she still found herself almost in the back of the room. *Now I see what the rush is to get to this class early.* By the time the older student finished setting up the projection equipment, freshmen and a few sophomores filled the room. Although she had been one of the tallest girls in high school, she felt tensely aware of how much older and more assured everyone else seemed. She was relieved that her sixteenth birthday had passed last Sunday. No one here needed to know how young she felt today.

Sandra had looked ahead in the textbook for University Writing, one of the required general education courses. She saw nothing unfamiliar. The style sheet for academic writing was a little different from the Associated Press guidebook she had used at the *Madison Messenger,* the local newspaper in London, Ohio. However, the principles of research and exposition were the same.

The graduate assistant went to the lectern and began the lecture for the day. She was glad that she had read ahead, because when he left the microphone to change transparencies on the projector, he kept talking, so only the front rows could hear him. After about twenty minutes, many students had taken out magazines. A few had fallen asleep.

Not sure that she could get away with such brazen inattention, Sandra forced herself to follow the lecture. The graduate student seemed to be following the textbook closely, so she took no notes the first day.

***

By the third week, she had figured out which classes required that she take notes, and which consisted of lectures that regurgitated the textbooks. The graduate assistant at that first class turned out to be a published author in his first teaching experience. After the third meeting, he paid more attention to his presentation and developed a sense of his audience. By the time wet leaves made walking to class a treacherous adventure, she found herself enjoying all her classes.

Sandra lived with the Menendez family, long-time friends and neighbors of the Billingsleys when Sandra's father played with the Army Field Band. Selena was a junior in high school, and the same age as Sandra. They had been best friends until the Billingsleys moved to Ohio when Sandra was in middle school. Selena's room included a bunk bed from the days when she and her older brother shared a room.

Music reigned in the Menendez family. Arturo and Maria were, respectively, the lead bassoonist and clarinetist in the National Symphony, and Selena seemed headed for great things with her violin. She played first violin for her high school orchestra but also worked with a local chamber quartet that was gaining a following in the DC metropolitan area. At sixteen, she had already cut two records with the group.

Sandra played viola but remained in awe of how much her friend had grown as a musician. Still, the duets coming from Selena's room in the evenings told the two grown-ups that neither girl was holding the other back. The violist in Selena's quartet occasionally played with the Richmond Symphony. When she was out of town, the quartet invited Sandra to sit in for their rehearsals.

***

A light snow, the first of the winter, covered the ground as Sandra crossed the sidewalk from the bus stop to Union Station. She watched the winter wonderland deepen as the *National Limited* carried her to Columbus, Ohio, on her first Christmas vacation. After eating the sandwich that she had packed, she took out the Amanda Cross mystery she brought with her.

Somewhere in the dark night, she nodded off. She dreamed of chasing Kate Fansler through the Berkshires, waking up the next day an hour from Columbus.

Stepping onto the platform, she looked for her parents but saw no one she knew.

"Hey, Sandra!"

She whirled to the right to see Bill Southern's messy brown hair over the crowd.

"Hi, Bill, what are you doing here?"

"You sent me the academic schedule. I figured you'd be coming in today, so I told your folks I would pick you up on my way home." Bill attended Ohio State University in Columbus. He had graduated from London High School with Sandra the spring before. "Your dad is coming for Marty tomorrow, so he was grateful for the help."

"Well, thanks!"

He took the suitcase from her hand and pointed to the rusty pickup truck at the far end of the parking lot. "It works just fine, but I can't afford the bodywork."

"I know." She pulled herself into the passenger's side while he tossed her suitcase in the bed. "We were never stranded on our dates."

The ride to the Billingsley farm flashed by as the two friends exchanged observations of their respective first semesters. They seemed to have the same list of required general courses before they could declare their majors. Bill planned to major in journalism, Sandra in Fine Art.

With a promise to go out the next day, Sandra jumped from the truck and pulled her suitcase from the truck bed. Bill sped off as her parents came to the porch. Sandra ran up the steps and hugged them both.

"Bill could have come in," said Marcia.

"He's running behind getting home. He'll be here tomorrow."

Her father took the suitcase and held the door. Sandra paused in the hall before taking off her shoes and coat.

"I'm glad I went away this semester, because it helped me understand how much I love this place."

"Welcome home," said Martin. He looked out the open door. "Here come James and Arnold. Be prepared to repeat everything tomorrow when Marty gets here."

Sandra's two younger brothers pounded up the steps and crashed into the house. Much hugging and slapping as they shed their coats and shoes.

It felt good to be home.

***

A week later, Sandra had a rare moment alone with her mother. They took mugs of hot coffee up to the studio, where they both enjoyed sitting among their paintings and looking out the large windows. Here Marcia, the art teacher at London High School, spent her few free hours each week. The walls and easels carried her work, but also a fair number of Sandra's paintings, many of which were homework assignments. The young woman called them her "commissions." It was a joke, but those paintings, along with her writing and sketching for the local newspaper, did win her a full scholarship to the George Washington University.

"I'm surprised you haven't been able to paint or draw since you left," said Marcia, as they basked in the sunlight coming horizontally through the western window. "I guess I shouldn't be, with all the foundation courses you need for a liberal arts degree."

"That's true. It's also giving us a chance to observe what's available before we have to declare a major."

"Aren't you going to take Fine Art?"

"Yes, but when I got there, I found out that they have three majors in the field: Fine Art, Art History, and both."

"Sounds like one is art and the other is writing about it."

"Not quite. The Art History still has a lot of hands-on painting, drawing, and even sculpture. But I think only the Fine Arts majors actually have to put on an exhibit; the Art History majors present theses and research."

"Interesting." She sipped her coffee. "Your friend Karen is doing very well, you know."

"She loves your class best. I'm not surprised."

"If she keeps excelling like this, I'll recommend she apply for scholarships to some of the better programs."

"Samara is hanging her pictures around the house along with hers." Samara Majid, now Samara Monroe, was an acclaimed artist and formerly a professor at GW.

Marcia glanced over Sandra's head. "Look at that winter scene. It's like another window in the wall on a day like this." They stood to admire Sandra's painting. "You didn't do this one for class."

"No, this was for me. What do you think?"

"Tell me about it."

"It's not a window, and that's not our farm. But it was a day like this at the Marshall farm up the road.

"That's Alice Marshall trudging home in the snow from the bus stop. I got this glimpse as the bus pulled away."

"She seems broken, like she's crying."

"She was. Michael Anderson dumped her in a dramatic show at lunch that day. Called her a bunch of unkind things and waltzed out with that new girl from Louisiana on his arm. Louise Callafont."

"I heard about that in the teacher's lounge. It was pretty dramatic."

"Yes. Alice was devastated. The teachers had to pull her out of the girl's bathroom twice."

Marcia peered closely then backed up. "Why are the footsteps in the snow like that? Her stride is lengthening. And are her hands clenched?"

"Yes. I'm glad you can see that. Her slump is coming up, but that's harder to show in a snap moment like this. I was imagining her already rising from this. Alice was deeply in love—in thrall maybe—but she was no shrinking violet. After the shock wore off that night, she called me.

"When Michael the bozo gets over the flashy new girl, he'll be sorry. Alice is her own girl."

"Quite a story. It came true, you know."

"It did?"

"By the time everyone came back from summer vacation, Louise was going with Zeke Armistead, who is captain of the basketball team now."

While Sandra told her mother how the painting came to be, the sun set, leaving the room in darkness. Marcia turned on a table lamp.

"Sandra, sometimes, I think you like the stories better than the pictures."

She walked downstairs to start supper.

Sandra felt a sudden emotion, but she was not sure what. Not hurt or even anything negative. An epiphany maybe. She stared at the painting for a while longer, then turned off the lamp and joined her mother in the kitchen.

***

The cherry blossoms bloomed in a more brilliant display than any in the memory of most Washingtonians, attracting a bumper crop of tourists. Sandra relished the fresh air as she crossed E Street and entered the Corcoran School of Art.

Inside, she climbed to the office of her assigned undergraduate advisor. Professor Andrews had gotten to know the "farm girl from Ohio" rather better than her other charges, but she never seemed to mind a visit or a meeting with Sandra.

For her part, Sandra was delighted to have the thirty-something artist and scholar as her advisor. Known for breaking glass ceilings, Maureen Andrews was one the youngest tenured professors and one of the few women at the school. GW was ahead of the curve on diversifying its faculty, but serious change was still in the future.

When Sandra asked to load up her second semester, Professor Andrews had supported her and fought the men who thought that it was too much work for a freshman. The precocious sixteen-year-old reminded Maureen of herself, though she did not admit it. Now, Sandra's grade point average was proving her right.

"Professor Andrews, thank you for seeing me."

"It's office hours anyway, but it's always a pleasure to see you. What can I help you with today?"

"Is there any reason I can't declare my major this semester?"

"No, not really. You will have all the required general courses completed by May. I sort of expected something like this. Fine Arts, right?"

"Well, that's a maybe. I'm asking because the brochure for the second year in Rome notes that applicants must have a declared and accepted major."

"Ah, you want to go to the American Academy."

"Yes, ma'am."

"Well, that's right. We have just enough time to get you in a major."

"About the Fine Arts major. I have been studying the course descriptions for all three majors, and I think I would do better in Art History."

"Fine Arts and Art History?"

"No. Just Art History."

"With your skill you could do the double one."

"Maybe, but as my mother noted last Christmas, I enjoy the stories behind the pictures more. That sounds like art history to me."

"I agree. And the way you write, I think you'll be very good at it." She opened a drawer in her desk and removed a form. "Shall we start the application process now?"

***

Sandra forced down the bubbles that wanted to escape her stomach as she handed her boarding pass to the flight attendant. She figured that she looked as pale as Susan and Ann ahead of her. This was their first flight, too.

On the other hand, Mary looked totally calm. Her parents had taken her to England last summer as a high school graduation present. Under the nonchalance, she shared the intense excitement of the other girls, embarking on their first adventure abroad without their families.

The four rising sophomores had been assigned an apartment in Rome together near the American Academy. For two semesters, they would walk to the American Academy overlooking the city from the Janiculum Hill across the Tiber.

Sandra would have had her first argument with her mother if the rates for long-distance phone calls had allowed it. Instead, she had written to her parents, to the editor of the *Madison Messenger,* to Samara Monroe, and completed scholarship application forms to a dozen donors. As a result, she had gathered enough support to pay for her room and board, and the plane ticket one-way. She was prepared to take a ship to return or find a job to save up the fare. She had learned that she could stay another year, if necessary, while keeping her undergraduate enrollment at GW.

The four young women had taken the train from Washington to New York to catch the nonstop Pan American flight to Rome. The other three girls had talked almost incessantly about the dreamy Italian men they expected to meet. Being two years younger and not having dated anyone but Bill Southern, Sandra contributed little to that conversation…

Sandra read the flight safety card carefully and listened attentively to the instructions from the flight crew. The descriptions of the correct brace positions and what to do if the oxygen masks dropped from the ceiling did nothing to settle her anxiety.

A half hour later, they let themselves relax in the incessant noise after the aircraft settled out at altitude. Sandra spent the first hour staring with wonder at the brilliant tops of the puffy clouds and the intensity of the blue sky. She tried to read for a while, but after the in-flight dinner (much better than she expected), she fell asleep. When the aircraft banked into a turn she started awake, a panic rising in her throat.

Looking out the window, she saw a vast, dark green plain extending to the white coastline. Glistening in the morning sun, the Eternal City glowed in golden hues, and the EUR World Exhibition shone with white marble buildings rising from the fields.

Sandra gasped and held her breath. All she had read and studied had not prepared for the pull she felt.

Instantly, hopelessly, and forever, Sandra Billingsley fell in love.

Internship

SANDRA BILLINGSLEY took a sip of Frascati, puckered her mouth, and shook her head. *It's true,* she thought, *it doesn't travel.* She stood and poured the white wine down the sink. She reached for the bottle of red Grottaferrata next to the bread box and poured a glass of something she knew.

Back at the kitchen table, she worked on the letter to her mother. The last phone call had not gone so well. Marcia Billingsley seemed to go on forever about Sandra being alone in Rome and not having family or a man to protect her. Sandra had bitten her tongue. *She's the art teacher; she should be excited for me.* When Sandra had tried to tell her about the paintings at the Capitoline Museum, her mother had interrupted twice. Her father had gone to collect Martin at the Columbus train station. Marty had a thirty-day leave between duty stations and was stopping home on his way from California to Virginia.

Phone calls were expensive, and it did not help that her parents were paying for it. She still felt the need to keep it short and to say something nice to everyone at home. She thought a while, then wrote,

Dear Mom,

Thank you for calling last night. I love to hear your voice. It's a shame that intercontinental service is so expensive, because I feel bad if I don't get to talk to everyone. I didn't know about Marty coming home and Dad not being there. In the future, let's propose a day for the phone call, so we can plan on being there. I'll start: I have classes during the day for another week. I'll have to let you know after that, because there are some very interesting job opportunities here in summer, and I might take one. That can be my news on the first call. In any case, I'm almost always here at home in the evening, and if we have a phone call planned, I won't go out that night. When would you like me to be available here, and who will be home there?

As I was saying on the phone, the Capitoline Museum is a treasure. Even if I weren't an art history student, the Campidoglio is such a delightfully cool place even on the hottest days, especially after climbing all those stairs. I know you know what I mean. The Borghese is still my favorite, even though the Vatican Museum is the most famous. My student ID card gets me into all of them for free, so I want to take full advantage of it. The ticket prices later will be terrible!

Please tell Samara that I stop at the <u>Dama con Liocorno</u> every time I go to the Borghese. I love to spend time sitting in front of it. Looking into that picture now, I not only imagine the life of the young woman, but I picture the woman in <u>Bride of the Chief</u>, and I think of Samara and you, and all the beautiful art we have shared in our homes and our conversations. You two are treasures, believe me, and it makes me very happy (and proud) to be your daughter and a friend to her and Karen.

Karen writes about every other week, which is wonderful. Between you and her, I am the envy of the others in the house. So much mail, they think!

Mom, when I tell you that I have no boys in my life, it's not that I don't have anyone at all. There are only four women here in the GW house, and the guys are fun, smart, and our ages (well, almost, since I <u>am</u> two years younger than everyone). Through my friends here, I've met several very nice Italian men, too. We go out together and we have a good time. In the house, we help each other with our projects. The Italian men try to be as charming as possible, but I get a little impatient, because they want to practice their English, so I can't ever improve my Italian! Thanks to Dad's voice lessons, at least I can pronounce it convincingly.

Remember Sonja Sankar in my class at GW? She wrote to tell me that she hopes to come to Rome next year for this same program. I might see her if she comes early.

Please let me know about the idea of scheduling the phone calls. Give Dad a big hug and kiss, and swat Jim and Arnie for me – lovingly, of course.

Your loving daughter,
Sandra.

She addressed the envelope and set it all aside to re-read before sealing it. The Grottaferrata went well with the *porchetta* sandwich that she had made on a *ciriola*, a Roman type of short baguette. She finished her lunch, washed the dishes, and went to her room to change. Cesare wanted to go to the American movie in English at the Fiammetta Theater near the American Embassy. She wanted to buy a copy of the *Rome Daily American* newspaper at the *Stars and Stripes* bookstore and look for a copy of *Christ Stopped at*

Eboli in the US Information Service library. They had made a date for the early showing.

An hour later, she hopped off the number sixty bus and walked up the Via Veneto to the Embassy Annex, where the bookstore and the library were. It was late May, but it was already hot downtown, probably as much from the traffic as from the sun on the buildings. The air-conditioned annex felt like a walk-in freezer when she stepped through the outside doors.

She was lucky to get the last copy of the newspaper, and the USIS library did not carry books by Italian authors, even in English. The librarian, however, knew that the American Catholic church, Santa Susanna, operated a lending library on the top floor of their education wing. That might be the place to find Carlo Levi's book. Otherwise, she'd have to buy it at an English-language bookstore.

Standing in the hallway with the newspaper, Sandra looked at her watch. A whole hour until her date with Cesare. Heavy interior doors led into the rest of the building, where she knew everyone worked. Curious about what might be there, she pushed her way through the doors.

In the middle of a marble-floored lobby, she was stunned by the two grand staircases that rose on either side. Rococo friezes and sculptured windows adorned the walls leading up to the offices on the five floors above her. Directly in front of her was the counter of the Army Post Office, which handled the diplomatic mail as well as the mail for the hundreds of military and civilian personnel and their families connected with the Embassy or the Military Advisory Assistance Group (MAAG). The unmistakable smell of a burger joint wafted up the stairs from the basement. Someone had told her that there was an American-style grill down there.

A large bulletin board to the right of the mail counter caught her attention. She walked closer and noticed the usual top ten wanted posters from the FBI, two of which she recognized from the post office back home in Ohio. There were all sorts of notices, and, to her surprise, job postings.

One notice advertised a summer internship with the FBI Liaison Office, Room 335, MAAG. Nothing on the advertisement seemed unfamiliar; she had done all those things in the newsroom at the *Madison Messenger* in high school. She copied the phone number and the point of contact at the Civilian Personnel Office and made note of the required forms. The CPO was around the corner from the Post Office, so she stopped by to pick up the forms, and put them in her purse.

Cesare was waiting at a café table outside Doney's bar on the Via Veneto, two blocks up the street from the Embassy. Sandra knew that he (or his family) was well-off, but still, meeting her at Doney's had to be showing off. She knew he didn't own a car or a scooter.

He sprang to his feet as she approached and pulled her in to kiss her on the cheek. After nine months in Italy, she was still getting used to kissing as a simple greeting, but she liked it. Sometimes, she recognized a hunger in men's eyes, and it made her wonder if there were more kissing of a different type waiting for her.

They ordered two espressos, and he signaled for the bill as the server left.

"We have plenty of time, but *Cleopatra* is a first-run show. I am sure that it will be packed."

Sandra agreed. They downed their coffees quickly, Italian-style. He left enough to cover them and the tip and took her hand as they stood.

Passing the other tables on their way, Sandra noticed the approving stares of the other patrons. Cesare stood a little taller than she, with shiny black hair that he kept well-glued back. With his Roman nose, high cheekbones, and dark eyes, he was a pleasure to look at, and he had the figure of the Roman statues that Sandra had admired throughout the city. No wonder, then, that the women let their stares linger.

But what surprised her was the admiration of their partners. Sandra felt almost embarrassed by the shameless staring of the men, who even smiled and nodded as she went by. Taller than most Italians, with powerful shoulders and long blonde hair, she did not realize just how exotic her appearance was, until Cesare explained it to her last week.

"You are exciting to watch, Sandra. It is very exciting. The men, they appreciate you as something rare and beautiful, which you are."

"And you?"

"I won't lie. I see you as exciting, but also – what's the word?"

"Sexy?"

"No. I mean, yes. Sexy is what I mean by exciting. But you have other quality. Strength, *carattere*. Yes, character! I not only like to be your friend, but I would be afraid to be your enemy."

Unable to process that, Sandra walked silently with him as they passed in front of the Embassy.

"You are insulted? I am sorry."

"No, no, not at all." She squeezed his arm. "I'm flattered but also surprised. I'm not used to attention from men. It's new and different."

"You are a beautiful woman, Sandra, you must be used to the looks."

"I'm just a girl, Cesare. I'm not used to it at all."

"You are a university student, like me."

"Yes, there's that." She tugged on his arm and lengthened her stride.

At the Fiammetta, they were a half-hour early, but the line wrapped around the block. They found seats in the back just before the theater darkened.

Cesare seemed as taken by Elizabeth Taylor and the epic cinematography as everyone else, but he occasionally muttered softly about a bad translation in the Italian subtitles. *His English really is good,* Sandra thought, *he just can't speak as fluently as he would like.* For her part, she could not have read the subtitles in the brief times they displayed, without the help from the English dialogue.

When he slid his arm behind her back, he asked, "*permesso?*" as if seeking permission to enter a home. Sandra felt a thrill at this attention but was also touched by his shyness and courtesy. No boy had ever asked before grabbing her or trying to hug her.

She reached up with her hand from the side away from him, and pulled his arm over, leaning into the side of his chest. He squeezed her shoulder, and she could have sworn that he sighed.

This felt so right, to snuggle with a handsome man in the dark. And a great movie, too. During the credits, he lifted the hand closest to him to his lips.

"You are special, Sandra. *Ti voglio bene.*"

Before she could say anything, the lights came on. They stood and filed out with the other patrons. The next crowd was already pressing at the doors at the back of the theater.

"Will you have supper with me?"

"Yes. Where?"

"I have ideas, but do you have a preference?"

"Do you like Chinese food?"

"I've never had it."

"Then let's try it. The China Garden is just across the street."

"The PanAm building?"

"The penthouse. Top floor."

"Oh. It's my city, and I never knew." He took her hand and walked with the excitement of a child on a new playground.

After egg rolls, she taught him how to use chopsticks, which he surprised himself by learning quickly. The servers beamed appreciatively at his efforts.

After supper, they walked up the Via Veneto. Sandra felt a growing anticipation, wondering if the evening could be more perfect. Heat was still radiating from the asphalt and the buildings, but not so much that the breeze did not keep it under control. Walking through the ancient Roman wall at the Porta Pinciana, they walked into the Borghese Garden. Cesare turned left as Sandra turned right, and they jerked hands.

"Sorry!" They said together, then laughed.

"Where are you going?" he asked.

"It's a habit. I spend so much time in the Borghese Museum that I started that way without thinking. Where were you going?"

"The Pincio. Have you been there?"

"Only to pass by on the bus. I've been to the Spanish Steps and the Trinità dei Monti."

"Close, but the buildings get in the way. Come."

He led her through the gardens, past the water clock and out to the overlook by the Villa Medici. The Janiculum Hill to the left of Saint Peter's Basilica resembled a dark monster sliding between the twinkling stars above and the city lights below.

"I think I live – over there." She pointed to the left end of the darkness.

"Yes. Me, too."

"Do you have your own place?"

"Oh, no. I am just a university student, too. I won't need my own place until I marry."

"Are your parents home with you?"

"Yes, and my two sisters."

"How old are they?"

"Seventeen and sixteen."

Sandra did not feel like mentioning that she was his sister's age.

"What if you don't find the right woman before, say, you're thirty or forty?"

"That does not matter, does it? A man leaves his mother and clings to his wife."

"You've never wanted to live alone?"

"How could I? Why would I?" She could hear the amazement in his voice. "I can't cook or clean a house. I don't know how to buy food or mend clothes or those things that women do."

"Wouldn't servants do them, too?"

"It's not the same. And what would I say to the servants? The *signora* runs the household. She tells the servants what to do."

Sandra thought immediately of an elderly English bachelor with his manservant and housekeeper but decided not to bring it up.

"This is a lovely view. So romantic."

"Yes, it is. You like Roma?"

"More than you know. Do you come here often?"

"No. Only when I meet someone special—like you."

They looked at the city for a few moments, then faced each other. As if rehearsed, they kissed with exactly the same level of gentleness, then pulled apart. She moved her arms farther behind him, and he hugged her closely. This time, the mouths met with passion and need. Sandra had never had anything feel so *right* in her life.

With their arms around each other's waist, they turned back to the view.

"Cesare, what does *ti voglio bene* mean? It's in songs, and you said that to me in the theater."

"I love you."

"Isn't that *ti amo*?"

"It's different. A friend says *ti voglio bene,* but mothers and spouses say *ti amo.*"

"So, it's more than 'I wish you well'?"

"That's the translation, but it's much more. There's loyalty and friendship in addition to love."

"That's beautiful."

"It's a beautiful language."

"*Perché non parliamo mai in italiano?*" Why don't we ever speak in Italian? She felt clumsy as she formed the words.

"Because I need to speak the English."

"What about me?"

"Your Italian is fine. What do you need?"

"For one, practice. For another, I like the sound of it, especially when you speak it."

He took her arm, and they walked toward the Trinità dei Monti.

"I want to go to America, Sandra. I need the English."

"And I want to study here. I need Italian."

"You can always find a husband with your English, but I need to speak better to succeed in America."

Sandra stopped and turned him toward her.

"Cesare, I am not attending university to find a husband. Why would you say that?"

"But it is normal. All the girls I know want the husband. There are better men at university, so they go, too."

After an initial flare of anger, she stood there, stunned. The honesty in his face and the sincerity in his voice disarmed her. Suppressing an urge to stomp off, she took his arm and started them walking again.

"You will need to learn more than English to succeed in America, Cesare."

From the Trinità dei Monti, they looked down at the Piazza di Spagna and the upscale shopping streets leading from it. The cars and people milled about the fountain like insects on a fallen piece of watermelon. They started down in silence.

"I can take the number forty-four bus home. You?"

"Same. I get off at Cavalleggeri. You go on to Trastevere, no?"

"Yes."

"Shall we shop the windows before we go back?"

"Actually, I need to finish a paper to present tomorrow. Let's do the shops when we don't have classes the next day."

"Okay. I will call you."

The bus was approaching the stop near the fountain when they reached it. They exchanged details on when their respective terms ended, and Sandra assured him that she was not planning to return to America right away. After the bus crossed the Tiber River and entered the tunnel, he rose to go to the door.

"Thank you for a wonderful evening, Cesare. *Arrivederci a presto.*" They squeezed hands, and he stepped off the bus.

***

"All hail, Cleopatra! How's Caesar?" Mary gave a big wink-wink, while Susan giggled. Ann was laying out the dishes while Mary poured the spaghetti into the colander. Susan turned the gas off under the sauce.

"Great. It was historically accurate and very well-presented."

They guffawed.

"Not the movie, dummy. Cesare!" Mary said with mock disgust. Sandra grinned so that Mary would know that she got it.

"He was fine, too. We almost didn't get in, so we had to sit in the back."

"I could handle the back row with him," said Susan.

"Yeah. We did snuggle a little, but the movie really was good. Afterward we walked to the Pincio. Then caught the bus from the Piazza di Spagna."

"That's a lot of walking." Ann was from New York City.

"About from the barn to the mailbox in Ohio," said Sandra. "Thanks, Ann, but we ate. I'll pour." She took four glasses from the cabinet and put away the plate that Ann gave her.

"So, you gonna see him again?"

"I think so." Sandra uncorked the Grottaferrata and poured wine for everyone. "Tell me, why do these guys date us? I mean, most of them are handsome and cool, but sometimes, they say some of the most clueless things."

"That's easy," said Susan. "Green card."

"Immigration?"

"Yes. The easiest way to get to the US is to marry an American. Some of them will do anything for that. Unlike here, we have divorce in the US, so they don't care if it doesn't work out."

"That's terrible!"

Mary finished dishing out the spaghetti. She motioned for them to sit, while Mary spooned the sauce onto the steaming al dente pasta.

"Sandra, sometimes you seem kind of clueless yourself. I mean, how many guys have you dated here?"

"Cesare is the fourth. He is really charming. I like him."

"And has any of them *not* mentioned going to America?"

Sandra thought. "I see what you mean." She grinned at them. "At least Cesare kissed me *before* mentioning America." They laughed.

In bed that night, Sandra went over the evening in her mind. She would have loved to snuggle with Cesare all night. But when she considered exactly what he had revealed as they stood at the Pincio, she felt a deep sadness. She hoped he would call; she didn't have his number, and she would not have wanted to talk to his mother or father, yet.

***

Cesare did not call, but Sandra could not dwell on it at first. Presenting papers and the oral examinations at the end of the term consumed her attention. She thought of him on her way from one class to the other, and briefly before falling asleep exhausted each night. Meanwhile, she completed the Civil Service application and the security clearance forms for a background check and delivered them to the CPO in the Annex.

The day after the last test, the phone rang in the apartment. Ann got it.

"No, but she's here… Sandra, it's for you!"

"*Pronto, con chi parlo?*"

"It's an American, Sandra!" Ann shouted.

"Your friend is right, Miss Billingsley." He chuckled softly. "This is Special Agent Redwood of the FBI. You applied for our summer internship."

"Yes, sir."

"I like the way you answer the phone. Could you come in for an interview?"

"Your office?"

"If you don't mind. Do you know where it is?"

"Room 335 in the Annex."

"Exactly. Would four o'clock today or tomorrow be suitable?"

"Today is fine, sir. Do you want me to bring anything?"

"Let's hope for the best. Bring your passport, stateside driver's license if you have one, and a nice smile for the security badge photo."

"Thank you, sir. I'll be there."

She cradled the handset and turned to Ann and Mary. "It's a job interview at the Annex. I may not have to go home!"

They gathered around and hugged her. Two hours later, they wished her good luck and watched her walk to the bus.

***

The interview was almost a formality. Three students had applied, but only Sandra could type, speak some Italian, and operate the telex and the fax machine, and much to the surprise of the FBI agent and his secretary, repair the new Xerox 660 photocopier. She had learned to repair most of the quirky failures of the machine in the *Messenger* newsroom. That she was familiar with police procedures and the criminal justice system was a bonus.

None of the four women in the apartment wanted to go back to the United States, so they convinced the American Academy to let them sublet the place for the summer. Sandra's stipend as an FBI intern more than covered her share of the rent and her other costs.

***

One day in mid-August, Sandra came to work to find the reception area empty. Agent Redwood was at his desk, intently looking at a report, ear to the handset of his telephone. *Strange,* she thought, *he rarely leaves the door open.*

"Ah, Sandra, you're here. Good." He put down the handset and motioned her in. "Miranda is in the hospital. Can you cover the office, or should I ask for a temp?"

"I think I can handle it, sir."

"That's what I thought, but I wanted to ask you first. We'll close up this afternoon and go see her. She should be out of surgery by noon."

"What happened?"

"Collision on the Via Aurelia. One of those little three-wheel trucks tried to run around a flock of sheep and went head-on into Fulvio's car." Fulvio was Miranda O'Brien's current boyfriend. The relationship was getting serious.

"How is Fulvio?"

"He died at the scene." He paused. "Will you be okay?"

Sandra took a breath. "Of course. Anything you would like me to do first? Otherwise, I'll have a look at her desk notes and set up your schedule. I'll call across the street about our being out this afternoon." She knew the secretaries who worked for the senior leaders of the Embassy and the MAAG.

"Thanks." He beamed. "I knew you would rise to this. Do one thing, while I finish analyzing this report from the *Polizia*. Call down to CPO and ask Henry to come see me tomorrow."

"Do you want me to mention Miranda?"

"He already knows. If she can't come back to work for more than two weeks, we need to bring you on as a full-time temp."

"Yes, sir. I'll take care of it."

Salvator Mundi Hospital was on the Janiculum Hill, an oasis among the cool pine trees, where wealthy citizens of ancient Rome built their summer villas. It looked like a holiday resort in an elegant *palazzo*, but inside it had the bright glare and disinfectant smell of any fully equipped hospital.

The hospital let them see Miranda for a half-hour, but it was clear that she was not coming back to work. She would be evacuated to the United States in two weeks for reconstructive surgery and then rehabilitation in her hometown.

Jim Redwood considered his secretary silently as they stood there, his hand on hers, Sandra at his side.

"Miranda," he said, "what do I do without you? You were here when I arrived. You taught me this place."

"Not a problem, sir." She tilted her head slightly at Sandra. "My relief is already onboard."

"Sandra?"

"Of course, if she'll take the job, she'll be better than I was. She's even smarter."

"But I will need to go back to school at some point."

"Didn't you say you could stay out a year?"

"Yes."

"That should give this lazy son of a gun plenty of time to find the next secretary. You'll do fine."

"Oh, Miranda. I'll miss you."

"I'll be back, dear. Or maybe I'll come to see you in DC when I'm better."

The nurse coughed behind them. They each gave Miranda a gentle hug and turned to leave.

"Sandra?"

She turned back. "Yes."

"You'll need a place to live. I just renewed the lease on my apartment. Would you mind taking it over? Obviously, you can afford it; I could."

"Of course. Thank you, Miranda."

"The *padrone* will be delighted not to have to find a new tenant."

Jim drove the embassy car back to the Annex.

"What time is Henry coming up?"

"Tomorrow at ten."

"You want the job?"

"The circumstances break my heart, but, yes, I have been trying to find a regular job all summer."

"It's yours. Welcome aboard, Signorina Billingsley."

Sketches

SANDRA CLIMBED THE STAIRS to Room 335 of the American Embassy Annex in Rome. She paused at the closed door to the FBI Liaison Office. *That's odd,* she thought. *Miranda is usually in early.* Then the reason for the closed door hit her like a flash flood in a gully.

Miranda was not coming back.

Sandra's supervisor had almost died in a car collision. Her fiancé, the driver, did perish. Miranda would be released next week for medical evacuation to the United States. She probably would not return.

As she groped in her purse for the keys, Sandra's throat closed, and the grief she had repressed for a week rose in her chest. Quickly, she entered the office, and found the light switches by feel. The tears ran while she finished pulling back the curtains, opening the inner office, and setting up the coffeemaker. She wiped her face with her handkerchief as she walked to the big oak desk in the main office to check the out-box. Nothing.

She stepped into the small room that held the coffeemaker, supplies and the shiny Xerox 660 photocopier. Sitting on the stool, she let herself shake and sob until there were no more tears. She wiped her face again, took a breath, and carried a cup of coffee back to her desk in the reception room.

The habit of arriving in class with her homework done worked well here. Having an empty in-box gave her time to gather her thoughts and emotions before her boss showed up.

Last week, Miranda had been that boss. Sandra had been a teenage summer intern trying to find a gig to keep herself in Italy for a year abroad before she returned to her art history major at the George Washington University. Overnight, she became the full-time secretary of the legendary Special Agent James Redwood.

Filling Miranda O'Brien's shoes scared the hell out of her.

To the *Polizia di Stato* state police, the *Carabinieri* military police, and the *Guardia di Finanza* of the Treasury Ministry, Sandra's boss represented the seventeen-thousand police agencies of the United States. The small office formed part of the MAAG, which had helped Italy and the other countries of Western Europe rebuild after World War II. The Marshall Plan had been a success, but the winding down would take a few years. The FBI Liaison Office gave law enforcement professionals in both countries a direct channel to each other, a situation that the two Allies liked very much.

When she felt like this, Sandra would usually play her viola. But she had stashed it somewhere in the apartment while moving yesterday. Instead, she took the sketchbook from her bag and reached for her pencils. Closing her eyes, she pictured how she wanted to remember Miranda.

At nine o'clock, Special Agent Redwood walked in and stopped in the doorway.

"Grieving at last?"

"Yes, sir. I'm sorry."

"Don't be. I was wondering how you were holding it for so long. I haven't slept well for a week." He noticed the sketchbook. "What do you have there?"

"Some sketches. After I got started, I decided to use this one for a portrait to give to Miranda." Redwood took the page from her. Sandra had drawn Miranda at her desk, explaining something to Redwood, who stood behind her, scratching his head. It was clear from the feeling of the scene who really ran the office.

Redwood laughed. "That's perfect! I'm sure she'll love it."

"I'm glad you think so. Should I mail it or give it to her before they take her home?"

"She won't be able to do anything with it until after the reconstructive surgery in the States. We have her home address." He gave it back. "I forgot that you mentioned the sketch artist work in your job interview. This is very good, really."

"Thank you. It's handy for capturing scenes when one can't pull out a camera."

"Courts are like that here, too, and various other occasions, like diplomatic parties and meetings. We might be able to use your skills here."

Redwood moved toward his office, then paused.

"Now I'm thinking of that interview. Did you say you play viola?"

"It was in my resumé. I don't think it came up in the interview."

"Did you play in groups? Chamber music, maybe?"

"Dad made each of us learn a different instrument, so the family could provide quartets and sextets for Church and other things. And I was in orchestra at high school."

"Anything since leaving Ohio?"

"I rehearsed alone in my apartment in Washington. I'm looking forward to not having roommates again, so I can practice." Along with the job, Sandra had taken over Miranda's lease, which the older woman had just renewed before the collision.

"Mmm." He snapped out of his thought to look more directly at her. "We should install a mirror near the coffeemaker or somewhere. You might want to run to the ladies' and check your eyes." He smiled, then he went into the office.

When she got back from cleaning her face and reapplying her mascara, Sandra reviewed her sketches and made some notes about colors. Then she put them away and called down to the supply department about a small mirror.

***

Two days later, Agent Redwood was in a conference with two Carabinieri officers.

"Sandra, could you step inside, please? Leave the door open so we can watch."

Inside, Sandra stood at the door. The Carabiniere major, a solid, red-headed Celt, smiled. The lieutenant, not much older than Sandra's dates, stood stiffly. He looked at her with pleasure but seemed wary of drawing attention to himself.

"Sandra Billingsley," Redwood said, "this is Major Mascagni and Lieutenant Russo."

Sandra arched an eyebrow as she shook the major's hand. He sighed and smiled.

"Yes, *signorina*. A great uncle." He seemed pleased that she recognized the composer's name. The lieutenant shook her hand with a short, gentle jerk and stepped back.

Redwood motioned for them to sit. Sandra chose a chair that let her see the entrance to the offices.

"As you know, the Carabinieri provide security in the courts, like our bailiffs and sheriffs. We were discussing a problem they are having, and I thought of your skills." He nodded to the major.

Major Mascagni's English was excellent, with only a slight accent. "We are currently concerned about the notorious Mafia case you may have seen in the papers. Somehow, the defendants are getting word of things that we know they cannot receive in prison. We think that something is being passed or signaled during the hearings in court, but in our meetings, no one seems to be able to catch anything, or remember enough with everything going on to be able to explain what they thought they saw."

"How can I help?"

"When I mentioned that we wished that cameras were allowed in court so we could analyze the room, Agent Redwood mentioned your ability as a sketch artist."

"Sandra, could you sketch the court sessions for a few days? The Carabinieri and the others would go over them to see if it brings out something they're missing."

"Yes, sir. The whole room, I take it."

"That's right, and over a few days, so that they can look for patterns or things that don't change."

"I'd be happy to." She smiled at Redwood. "Can you run the coffeemaker without me?" The men laughed.

"I'll have Henry send Rosemary up while you're gone. You would come to work normally, then go to court and back from here."

"Want me to watch for anything in particular, also?"

"Of course," said the FBI agent. Turning to Mascagni, he said, "From what I have seen, she is very observant. If she asks about something, you should probably look into it."

"That would be helpful. Thank you."

They agreed that an unmarked car would pick up Sandra behind the Embassy at noon and return her to the office. She would fix up the sketches the same evening, and Agent Redwood would take them to the Carabinieri on his way home. That way, the security detail could use them the next day for their morning meeting.

After the Carabinieri left, the two Americans went to the coffeemaker.

"Rather scary compared to a burglary trial in Madison County court, sir."

"Much higher stakes, yes. If you can help them zero in on whatever is going on, we will have made some good friends. This trial could help us shut down major operations in New York and New Orleans in addition to Italy."

Each day, Sandra met the plainclothes policeman in the Fiat 600 at a different corner near the Embassy and walked to court from a different direction.

The architecture of the Palace of Justice and the courtroom stunned her at first. To get herself under control, she sketched the majestic room empty. Then she could concentrate.

The room seated several hundred, with dozens more standing in the back. She saw sketch artists next to the reporters in the press area, but they were clearly at a disadvantage, being in the front rows. They did not seem interested in what the crowd was doing, anyway.

The Carabinieri had arranged for Sandra to have a seat in a shallow balcony of sorts, which ran around the top of the room, normally used for maintaining the lights and cleaning the ceiling. She could see everyone, but she was also hidden from the people below. Even those who might see the top of her head could not see what she was doing.

On the fourth day, Major Mascagni called just as Agent Redwood walked in. He took the phone, standing at Sandra's desk. He held the microphone against his hand.

"He'd like you to attend the morning meeting with his team."

"He does know my Italian is limited, doesn't he?"

"Don't worry. He and Lieutenant Russo can help. I've heard your Italian on the phone. You'll do fine."

"Okay, then. I'd be happy to help."

Redwood spoke into the phone. "*Va bene, maggiore. Quindici minuti.*" Okay, major. Fifteen minutes. Then he hung up.

"That comment about the teams at different corners in the back got them wondering. You're a hit, young lady."

Sandra blushed and gathered her things.

"Do I come back here before court?"

"If they want to buy you lunch, feel free to let them bring you back after today's session."

"See you after court, then."

***

Tuesday morning, the news was full of the dramatic arrest of two dozen mafiosi in the courtroom, including two of the capo's senior lieutenants and the senior defense attorney. The event seemed to light a fire under the prosecuting magistrates: the defendants were found guilty by the end of the week.

On the last day, Sandra drew a sketch of the court delivering its verdict, with Major Mascagni and his men standing in full dress uniform at either end of the bench. She colored the drawing over the weekend.

On Monday, she had just started the coffeemaker and opened Redwood's door when Major Mascagni knocked on the door. In his hand he held an enormous bouquet in an elegant vase of hand-blown Murano glass. The blues and reds of the glass turned the light from the windows into stunning patterns on the walls, with the shadows of the stems in the middle.

"*Buon giorno, signorina.*" He placed the flowers on her desk. "The entire court security detachment is indebted to you. But anything else we could think of would break some ethics rule, so it will have to be flowers."

"Major, thank you. These are beautiful." Sandra's chest swelled with emotion. "I've never received flowers like these. Ever."

"I can't believe that a beautiful lady like you has not received flowers." Sandra knew from her dates that effusive compliments came naturally to Italian men, but it still felt strange.

"It's true. I'm just a girl from the Midwest. Boys there don't even think of anything like this."

The major looked at her with his lids half-closed. Then he opened his eyes.

"But I'll bet you thought of it, didn't you?"

She blushed. "Yes. I did, but I never expected it."

"Well, you deserve it. If we can do anything for you, just call." He put his business card on the desk. The home number was penned on it, too. "My wife's name is Angela, if you call me at home. She knows who you are."

Sandra was still blushing.

"Would you like some coffee?"

"Thank you, but we have another court case starting today. Perhaps we can meet another time outside the office."

"I would like that. To whom should I return the vase?"

"It's yours, signorina, from Romolo – Lieutenant Russo. He has relatives in Murano on his mother's side. That vase came straight from his uncle's factory. We had it flown down over the weekend."

Redwood walked in and paused in the doorway.

"I told you that you were a hit." He smiled. "I think Miranda had some leftover plant food somewhere."

"In the coffee cabinet. Thanks for reminding me."

"Oh, that explains that extremely bitter coffee I made myself once." He shook hands with Mascagni. "*Caffè?*"

"The signorina just offered. I must go to court. Another time, perhaps."

"I have something for you, Major." Sandra reached into her bag on the desk. "If Agent Redwood doesn't mind." She showed it to her boss, who looked at it, then nodded. She held it out to the Carabiniere.

"I can't —"

"Then please give it to – Angela, is that right? She can remember her hero by it."

He took the picture. Sandra thought he might cry.

"Now we have each been surprised. Thank you." He shook Redwood's hand and left quickly.

"You have a friend for life, Sandra."

"Was he about to cry?"

"Maybe. But not for himself." Redwood paused to look out the window to someplace far away, and maybe long ago. With a sigh, he returned his gaze to the young artist. "I could see a commander looking at his detachment. That picture captures how he feels about his men, Sandra.

"You have a rare gift there."

Music and Sketches

ON A SUNNY DAY IN MID-SEPTEMBER, Sandra was humming an aria from *Cavalleria Rusticana* when Special Agent Redwood came through the door. As important as the FBI Liaison Office was, tucked on the third floor of the American Embassy Annex in Rome, it was a small staff, just the two of them.

"You do know your music, don't you?"

"It was on the radio last night. The Easter Hymn aria stuck in my head."

He went to the coffeemaker and came out with a cup. "Are you rehearsing your viola again?"

"Yes, sir."

"I may have a non-paying gig for you. Do you have a date tomorrow?"

"No, sir. Social life has been quiet since school ended."

"How about dinner at our place? Arlene would love to play something besides duets with piano."

"She plays cello, doesn't she?"

"That's right. The NSO is the only thing she misses about our tours in Washington."

"Omigod! She played in the National Symphony?" Sandra pulled her jaw back up.

"Relax, Sandra. I'll be on piano. That levels the playing field. Besides, she's a music teacher, so she knows how to play with different levels. One of her students lives in the apartment below ours. He comes up with his violin anytime we tap a 'V' on the floor."

"Beethoven's Fifth Symphony?" asked Sandra.

"Right. Ernesto does not want to come for dinner or socialize. I think I intimidate him. But he would come play his violin all day if we let him. Arlene hopes he can win a place in the Santa Cecilia conservatory."

"Thank you, sir. I would love that. Can I help with dinner?"

"You could, but let's let Vittoria and Arlene figure it out this first time."

***

Thursday nights at the Redwood apartment in Vigna Clara became a habit. Sandra had played first chair in the London High School Orchestra in Ohio, but apart from that, she had no basis for comparison outside her family. Her father, a retired Army musician, must have held his four sons and her to a higher standard than she knew, because Arlene Redwood was enthusiastic about having a solid partner in the quartet.

After the second week, Sandra would go home with Agent Redwood, help cook, and take the bus to her apartment. He always offered to drive her home, but she preferred to take the bus. Rome was not a dangerous city at night.

Doug Redwood, a junior at Notre Dame International High School and a star basketball player, joined them for dinner occasionally. More often, he would come back late from basketball practice. He did his homework in his room while they played.

One Thursday, conversation strayed to the subject of dinner parties at the Embassy. From September to early January, it seemed that every embassy, private school and global corporation in town tried to get on the social calendar of the glitterati of the Eternal City.

"I swear, Jim, if we could think of an excuse, I would love for you to take someone else to those things." Arlene finished her wine.

"Is it that bad?" asked Sandra.

"Not really, but by December, it will be every Friday, Saturday and Sunday night, and I will be ready to scream."

Jim refilled their glasses. "I used to believe the scandal-mongering newspapers when the paparazzi photographed some diplomat with a young beauty on his arm." His eyes crinkled as he smiled. "Now I think maybe his wife paid for the escort service."

"Do you think you could get Sandra some time-and-a-half?" Arlene swished her glass toward the young secretary. "It would be overtime for her wouldn't it?"

"Being a policeman, I am one of the few men around who can show up without a lady on his arm. It would be assumed that I'm doing security. But not all the time."

Arlene sighed. "I know, but I just wish I could skip most of them."

A few minutes later, Jim pounded Morse code on the living room floor. Ernesto came up, and the quartet played Dvořák for two hours. Sandra toted her viola case and bag to the bus and stared dreamily at the lights on the Tiber River as she rode home.

***

The following week, Sandra was opening envelopes when Redwood walked in from lunch.

"I see what you mean about the dinner parties, sir." She waved the letter opener at a sizeable pile of cream-colored envelopes of heavy, expensive paper with a variety of colored coats of arms or corporate logos.

"I'll take those home, so Arlene and I can do triage on them. Would you please contact the ambassador and the general to see which are must-attend affairs, and which of those require our wives?"

"Yes, sir." She knew he meant the secretaries. The ambassador and the general commanding the MAAG wouldn't have a clue.

Two days later, Redwood called Sandra in to help prioritize the social invitations. Between them, they got the list that Arlene had to attend down to only four events: the Marine Corps Ball, and three dinners at the Villa Taverna, the American ambassador's residence.

The next day, when Redwood came in, Sandra passed him a cryptic message from the Cultural Attaché, who she knew was the CIA station chief in Rome. The FBI and the CIA had different missions, so they rarely had a reason to interact. However, the Redwoods and the Morrisons played tennis most weekends, and had become friends.

"Rosalie called. She said, 'remember the common players'."

"Oh, yes. I almost forgot. This one may be for you. Get us some coffee and come into the office. Close both doors, please."

When they were seated, Redwood sipped his coffee and considered the young woman across the conference table from him.

"This room has been swept. You know what Rosalie's boss does, don't you?"

"I'm not supposed to, but yes."

"I thought so. Nothing much escapes you."

"Thank you, sir. What can I do for you—or is it for Mr. Morrison?"

"Both, actually. You know about the three dinner parties at Villa Taverna."

"Yes, sir."

"There are some people on the guest list that neither the CIA nor the FBI can find a picture of. We suspect that one or more of them may not be who they are supposed to be. Does that make sense?"

"It does not surprise me, sir. Not after the Mafia trial last month."

"That trial is why your name came up. We'd like you to do another sketch job."

"At a dinner party?"

"I know, it's weird. We're still figuring out how to do this. At Villa Taverna, we could make a private room available for you to sketch while absenting yourself as little as possible. Do you think that would work?"

"Has no one been able to photograph them at all?"

"No. Security on them has been airtight since they came to Rome, and no one has been able to get near them. The only photographs we have found are ancient and unrecognizable."

"I guess I could do this. How many people?"

"Three men and one woman."

"That's doable, but how do we put me in the place? Am I to be a server or something?"

"No. The waiters are all men, so you would attract attention. I propose to escort you."

Sandra gasped. Then, she remembered the conversation last week.

"Was this Arlene's idea?"

"No, but she thinks it's great, and she'd be delighted."

"You probably can expect my next question."

"You haven't a thing to wear?" He chuckled.

"Yes, sir. I absolutely don't."

"Arlene thought you would say that. She would be happy to go shopping with you on a couple of afternoons or mornings, and help you pick out some suitable evening wear. I don't know why she won't lend you hers—"

"Because she's worn them, and all the women would immediately know who gave them to me."

Redwood grinned. "You may have a career in the diplomatic service if you want it, young lady."

"We are talking the Via del Corso, aren't we? I can't afford that kind of clothing."

"This is official business. We have funds for it."

"For most girls, this would be a fairy tale dream."

"Not for you?"

"I made my dress for the high school prom. This will be a new experience."

"Enjoy it, then. You know when the parties are. Call Arlene and set it up, then ask Rosemary to cover while you're out." He stood, and Sandra rose also.

"Aren't you worried about paparazzi?" Sandra had a vision of some horribly mocked-up photo of herself at a newsstand.

"Arlene's in on this, remember. Consider this: who is the only woman who would have a man's confidence besides his wife? Maybe instead of his wife?"

"His secretary."

"See? You're not just a pretty coed." He winked. "You'll be fine. It will make perfect sense to anyone who knows us."

***

Shopping with Arlene would forever remain one of the memorable experiences of Sandra's youth.

For a professional musician like Arlene, evening wear was a work uniform, so she could help Sandra pick gowns and dresses that would do double duty. Mostly black, with accessories to make them different, and a few shorter dresses in colors that set off Sandra's blond hair.

"But it's just one to three dinner parties—at night," Sandra protested when Arlene brought out the first afternoon cocktail dress.

"If this works, dear, you can count on Jim wanting to do this again, or maybe you'll need to go without him. I asked him, and he agreed to outfit you for future assignments. We might not get the checkbook next time."

Sandra smiled. "Let's do this, fairy godmother! Don't forget the glass slippers."

Arlene pointed out style features that would never go out of fashion, and places where small adjustments would easily keep the dress current. They took two different mornings to complete the assignment, including part of a day on the Via Condotti at the jewelry stores.

***

"You okay?" asked Redwood as they rode to the Villa Taverna from Vigna Clara.

"Scared spitless, sir, but I'll be okay—I think."

"Like I said in the house, you look stunning tonight. With your instincts, you'll be a hit."

She had been surprised when she found out that part of the planning was for her to change at the Redwood apartment and go to and from the events with Jim. Those who knew the Redwoods would also recognize that the special agent had his secretary on his arm, not some "pretty young thing." An unmarked army sedan with a driver delivered them and picked them up, which made them less conspicuous among the dignitaries alighting at the entrance to the residence. Sandra had taken her art supplies in her book bag to the residence earlier and been given the key to a room around the corner from the ladies' lounge. The door was behind a curtain, making it look like a closed window.

The butterflies threatened to make her burp or worse. She breathed deeply and slowly and reviewed the plan for the evening in her mind.

During the cocktail hour, Jim steered her to a corner where they could appear to chat and watch the guests entering.

"There's the first two. Both from the Egyptian Embassy." He looked at her until she nodded. "The one on the left is supposed to be Amir bin Pasha, a ridiculous name, and the taller one is Mahmoud abu Youseff." The two Egyptians went by, then he nudged her arm. "Mikhail Berwitz, Soviet Embassy. Morrison thinks he's GRU, but no one is sure." Soviet Military Intelligence.

Sandra saw a tall woman in a flame-red evening gown appear, with a man about her height. It was not obvious who was on whose arm. Her black hair shone in the light, and her skin was perfectly clear, but her face was not girlish. Nor was her figure. Most of the male heads in the room did a slight shift, some to stare, others to cover the movement before resuming conversation. The women acted as if they hadn't noticed, but every one of them covertly analyzed each detail of the new arrival.

"Let me guess. That's the woman."

"She is supposed to be Ariadne Sangemini, Contessa di Monforte, and her escort is a French attaché, one Gérard Moussine. We can't confirm anything about her, except that there is a title and an estate by that name in Cuneo province and another near Cassino. The French Embassy asked to put her on the guest list, using the cultural attaché's address."

"This will be an interesting evening. Should I engage and mingle, or hover and go draw?"

"Whatever feels comfortable."

"I'll mingle on the edges, get a good look, and try to draw before the dinner gong."

"Sounds like a plan. I'll double-check our seats. Meet you at the gong." And he was gone.

Suddenly Sandra felt very alone and terrified. Then she remembered what her father had said. "It's an act — all of it. So, play your role." Arlene had said something like that, too. Sandra took a breath and moved toward the server walking around with a tray of flutes of spumante sparkling wine. She kept the Egyptians and Russians in her peripheral view. Ariadne Sangemini's features were already burned in her brain.

Pretending to sip the spumante, Sandra eased toward the Soviet official, who was chatting with the

American Army attaché and his wife. The Russian's accent was impeccable—and American. Sandra studied him for a while, then moved toward the Egyptians, stopping to say hello to Steve Wolcowski, the American First Minister, and to thank the ambassador for the invitation. Both men were polite and kind, doing nothing to draw attention to her. That put her next to the Egyptians, who were chatting with each other and a short woman with a black shawl heavily embroidered with gold thread.

The shorter Egyptian man noticed her gaze.

"May I help you?"

"Sorry, I'm staring." She looked at the woman. "I was admiring your shawl. It's beautiful."

"Thank you, young lady," said the woman. "Mara Nasrin, and you?"

"Sandra. Sandra Billingsley. How do you do?"

"I am Amir bin Pasha, and this is my associate, Mahmoud abu Youssef." They shook hands. "You are American?"

"Yes. Are you with one of the embassies?"

"We are both from the Egyptian Embassy. Madame Nasrin is – what would you say?"

"A private party." She smiled enigmatically. "I came with Mahmoud here, actually."

"Well, I hope you have a wonderful time."

"You too, Miss Billingsley."

Sandra bobbed slightly and took her glass around the corner where no one could see her. She took a few deep breaths to recompose herself. Before withdrawing, she looked out on the room again, trying to take in the feeling of the place. There was something jarring about the people milling about under the Rococo friezes and the painted ceiling. *Like bad acting in a beautiful theatre,* she thought.

After checking the seating chart, she put her glass on a table in the hallway and disappeared into her "drawing room."

As she returned the sketchbook and the pencil case to her bag, she heard the chimes moving down the hall. She slipped out and went into the ladies' lounge before looking for her boss. He was easy to spot, flanked by a pair of gray-haired sisters or cousins, who came up to his shoulder. She walked toward them, with a smile.

"Ah, there you are." He turned to the ladies and introduced Sandra to them without explaining her role. They made polite noises.

"Have you seen the seating chart?" Sandra asked.

"Yes. Ladies, shall we dine?" He took Sandra's arm and walked to the side, so the two women could precede them into the dining room.

Sandra found herself across from Jim and seated between two elderly gentlemen. On her right was the head of the British Council, a former don at Oxford University with a specialty in Italian literature before 1700. To her left sat another academic, the dean of the American Academy, where the George Washington University operated its semester-abroad program in Rome. She had heard his name but had never had occasion to meet him when she was studying on the grounds of his school.

The dinner conversation allowed her to slip into a shared love of art history, the Italian Renaissance, and scholarship in general. Occasionally, Jim would catch her eye and smile appreciatively. He had the Contessa di

Monforte on one side and one of the two matrons on the other. The latter seemed quite taken with the French gentleman on her right, so Jim could listen to the Contessa most of the time. Sandra tried to spot the Russian and the two Egyptians, but they were on her side of the table.

The food was as expertly prepared and presented as the conversation with the two scholars. Sandra felt even more like Cinderella than she had shopping with Arlene. She was not ready when the ambassador rose and made his short remarks and led a couple of toasts. The guests rose. Most went to find their partners.

"I do hope we can meet again, Miss Billingsley," said the dean. "I have never been able to enjoy one of these dinners as much as I did tonight."

"Thank you, sir. That would be nice."

"We have scholarship programs at the Academy. You might try for one through your graduate school. They're not restricted to graduate students."

"I'll look into it. Thank you."

She excused herself from the two professors and went toward the ladies' lounge, slowing so Agent Redwood could catch up with her. They paused near the coat room to let the important guests leave first. Sandra gave the "drawing room" key to Jim, who passed it to one of the Marine guards near the entrance. Their driver brought the car to the end of the queue of departing limousines. The Marine appeared with Sandra's bag, and gave it to the driver while Sandra and Jim got in. The driver passed the bag back on the way to Vigna Clara.

It had been a long day. Arlene insisted that Sandra use the guest room and go home in the morning. Silence reigned over the apartment, as the young secretary fell into a happy, dreamy sleep.

***

The last Monday in November, Rosalie called Sandra at about eight-thirty in the morning.

"Tell your boss we have news on the common players."

"Got it. Thanks."

When he arrived, Redwood called Morrison from his office. He hung up in just a few seconds.

"Sandra, Walter Morrison is coming over. When he gets here, please join us and close the doors."

She had a fresh pot of coffee ready when the CIA station chief walked in. After they settled in the conference room, Morrison asked if the FBI agent had learned any more about Sangemini.

"Yes. It turned out that she was from Cuneo, and very well-connected. But Sandra here gave me the tip that led me to ask the right people." Sandra looked down.

"Why am I not surprised?" said Morrison. "What tip?"

"She said the woman reminded her of a painting that used to be in a Jesuit church in Monforte. Then she traced the descendants of the noblewoman in the portrait, and it led her to Sangemini's family. It turns out that the State Police has a thick file on her. She was a Monarchist until the Party folded, and she has been very influential in MSI circles since then. But always behind the scenes."

"General Arcibaldo's party."

"That's the one. She happens to own the building they use on Via della Scrofa. And she supported Arcibaldo for his seat in Parliament when he retired from the Carabinieri."

"Interesting. I can't believe that we had nothing on someone that important all this time." He shook his head.

"What do you have?" asked Redwood.

"We identified all three men, thanks to your drawings, Sandra. They were so good that we could run them through a facial recognition program that the National Security Agency (NSA) is developing, and we got perfect hits."

"Amazing what computers can do, eh?" said Redwood.

"Yes. And remember that the NSA program is still codeword classified. Don't ask for details."

"Of course. Well?"

"The Soviet is Colonel Viktor Pachinsky of the GRU. He is wanted in a dozen countries, including the US and Canada. He returned to Moscow last week.

"The two Egyptians are who they say they are. The surprise is that the woman with abu Yousseff is Mossad, the Israeli secret service. Thanks for including her in your drawings, Sandra. She came as his date, no name given. We would have missed her."

"She seemed like the most interesting person in the conversation, sir. I had to draw her or itch about it forever." She looked at both men. "If I may ask, why are you sharing this with me?"

Redwood answered. "Because you may see more of this kind of work. We applied to have your security clearances increased to Top Secret and SCI. As soon as you're briefed, we may be asking you to attend highly classified meetings or events and draw what you see. Interested?"

"Oh. Okay." She smiled, feeling a little embarrassed. Sensitive Compartmented Information was even more carefully guarded than Top Secret. "Thank you—I think?"

Part II – Joe

Fedhala

"THERE. FINISH UP, NURSE, THANK YOU." Her wide, brown eyes did not change expression as she waited for instructions. "Sorry. *Et voilà. Je vous laisse finir, madame.*"

"*Bien sûr, docteur. Allez vous reposer.*" Sure, doctor. Go get some rest. She reached for the bandage tape and began cleaning and covering the incision. She was the third nurse to assist him today. An American WAC, a Scottish nurse from the British Army, and this local civilian who volunteered. The patients were just as varied.

Jason Lockhart wiped the sweat from his brow with his bloody forearm and turned unsteadily to the wash basin in the corner of the tent. Another one saved. He cleaned up as best he could and staggered into the blinding sunshine to find his quarters. After the oppressive heat of the heavy medical tent, the wind off the Atlantic felt wonderful, in spite of the sand and salt spray that came with it.

He fell onto his cot fully clothed.

Someone shook his shoulder. Opening his eyes, he saw that it was dark.

"Napping on the job again, Lockhart?" Marcus MacAlan's cheerful Scottish brogue finished waking Jason up. "Come get some food. Then go back to sleep."

"What time is it?"

"Eighteen hundred. I think that's two bells of the second dogwatch to you swabbies." He grinned. "What's important is that the mess tent is still serving supper. I know you'll sleep through that and breakfast again if I don't watch out for you."

"Thanks, Marcus. You're a real friend."

"And you're a damn hero. You pulled sixteen men back from the brink today. It's the buzz all over the camp."

"That many? I lost count."

"I noticed. Now you finish cleaning up and change into something decent. Then let's eat."

Forty-five minutes later, Lieutenant Commander Jason J. Lockhart, MC, USN, emerged from the tent looking more like a naval officer than the blood-splattered, dark-eyed skeleton that had crept into it some three hours earlier. His friend Marcus, a surgeon attached to the British Army forces in the invasion, walked with him to the mess tent.

"About the only bright side to this operation is the food," Marcus said as they pointed to entrees on the line. "You Yanks have no idea how to set up an officers' mess in a tent, but at least you were smart enough to accept the French offer to send over their cooks."

"I agree. The cooks on our hospital ship are good, but this is special." They carried their portions of *coq au vin*, *flageolet verts* and *pommes de terre rissolées* to a table. The only thing missing was a good French wine, but it was an American operation, so no luck there.

"Aren't you on at midnight?" Jason asked as they tucked into the hot, dripping chicken.

"Aye, but I took a nap, and I'll take another before going on."

"I hope you have a dull shift."

"Thanks. I hear the battle was short-lived. Gave us lots of work now, but we should not have many trickling in after today."

"Any word on your replacement unit?" One of the two landing craft with medical teams on board took a hit from a French destroyer and sank. The Commander of the Central Force ordered the hospital ship to send over a surgeon with a nurse and some corpsmen to help until replacements could come from Gibraltar. That put Jason Lockhart and four others in the sand.

"Last word was two hours ago. The hospital in Gibraltar balked at losing a full surgical team, but they promised replacements in a week after General Patton threatened to visit them personally."

"I hear Old Blood and Guts is a real sweetie."

An hour later, the two tent mates were fast asleep.

***

In the morning, Jason awoke to the sound of bugles and shouts of soldiers. One of his corpsmen knocked outside.

"Doctor Lockhart, sir?"

"Yes, Williams, I'm awake. What's going on?"

"Breaking camp, sir. The Vichy surrendered. We're moving into the city."

"Fedhala? It's too small."

"Casablanca, sir. All three landings are consolidating there."

"Okay. Thanks. I'll be packed and out of here in a few minutes. Is Nurse Haines up?"

"Yes, sir. She already mustered the rest of us at the hospital tent."

Jason grinned. "Good. I'll be right out."

Marcus appeared as Jason shouldered his duffel and stepped outside.

"I hear that our humble home is disappearing."

"Aye, and it's the big city now." Marcus slapped Jason on the arm and went into the tent to pack.

At the hospital tent, Lieutenant Haines was checking on the wounded with the three corpsmen. When she saw Jason, she motioned him outside.

"Good morning, sir. I hope you slept well."

"Yes, nurse, thanks. I came straight here, but I probably should have stopped at the command tent."

"Did that already, sir." A head nurse in a big city hospital before the war, Beulah Haines was accustomed to handling young doctors as skillfully as she handled wounded gangsters, and now, soldiers. "Word is that all three Attack Forces will move overland to the Mediterranean Coast."

"And?"

"And we go with them. Apparently General Patton was impressed when he saw how many survived here in Fedhala." She caught the slight sag in Jason's face. "No good deed goes unpunished, sir." He snorted, and they joined the others to organize their part of the move as the tents came down around them.

***

Three weeks later, Jason was stitching the right leg of a ten-year-old boy in the operating tent near Tangiers. The other five boys were killed by a land mine where they were playing. Jason had managed to connect all the muscles in the leg and put everything back together. Beulah Haines helped him with the bandaging.

"He'll limp for the rest of his life, but hopefully not enough to slow him down." Jason looked up as an orderly walked in.

"Out of here!" Haines barked. "This is a sterile area."

"Sorry." The young private ducked back out and called in. "You've got mail! The postal clerk sent me to let you know, because we almost never get Navy mail."

The surgical team exchanged glances, then smiles. They cleaned up the operating area briskly and joined the Army surgical teams at mail call that afternoon.

"Here you go, Jason." Marcus MacAlan handed him a full canvas bag. "I saw it on the back of the truck with just your name on it. I wager the ship's mail room was overflowing with unclaimed mail for you five."

"I guess. Thanks." After all the mail was distributed, the two friends walked back to their tent, where Marcus pulled out a bottle of single malt whisky from his duffel and shared it with Jason as they opened their envelopes. Jason's mail was almost all from his brother, so he put the letters in chronological order. It was the first mail he had received since leaving the US three months earlier.

Ilion, New York

August 15, 1942

Dear Jace,
I have no idea where you are, when you'll get this, or what you're doing, but I hope you are safe and in a place where you can keep up with events at home as I write. Since

you left, everyone has been fine, more or less. Mother had a cold last month, but she got over it. Dad has been busy taking care of her, which is a big help to Carrie and me, because the gun factory has put us on 12-hour shifts. Carrie had to quit her job to be here for the twins. My overtime doesn't quite replace her income, but there's less and less to buy every week anyway. Thank God we have a garden.

I hope you beat the Krauts and get home soon. Mother, Dad, and Carrie join me in sending you our love. You are daily in our prayers.

Frank

"Seems like everything is stable at home." Jason took another sip of the Scotch. "This stuff is so smooth! Where does it come from?"

"A little still down the road from our house. Glen Fiddich."

Jason counted the letters again. There were three more.

Ilion, New York

September 1, 1942

Dear Jace,

The news is not good this time. Mother fell last week. She thought she was going up to her bedroom, but she was at the top of the stairs, not the bottom. She broke her right hip and her left forearm. Dad is with her in the hospital in Utica, helping to care for her. He drives back here to shower and shave and change his clothes. It feels like no one is home when I wake up after sleeping (I'm on the night shift), and the girls are at school. Most times, Carrie is shopping, out in the garden, or visiting Mother when I get up. Carrie is incredible. She gardens, repairs masonry and cabinetry, cooks, cleans, and keeps the twins under control by making them help. She has me show her things she doesn't know when I'm up, but then takes care of them herself after that. When I see the posters of Rosie the Riveter near the clock at the factory, I have to smile. Rosie has nothing on Carrie.

Mother is not well, but all we can do is pray now. Stay well yourself.

Frank

Jason tore open the next letter.

Ilion, New York

September 15, 1942

Dear Jace,

This is a terrible way to tell you, from so far away. Our parents have died. Mother passed away in the hospital three days ago. Dad was crying when he left. I have never seen him cry in my life. The police found his car by the side of the road, still running. He was slumped over the wheel. The doctors at the hospital think he had a heart attack. I've authorized an autopsy, but I don't know if I want the details. You might, though: it's your profession. So, I told them to go ahead.

Don't anyone ever tell me that you can't die of a broken heart. I am so sorry to have to write to you. It is taking me a while to write all this, because I keep stopping. I'm crying myself, sitting here alone, sharing this news.

There is so much to do, even as we try to process having them both gone so suddenly. Just this morning, word came down that some of us will be sent to Independence, Missouri, to expand the factory there. Meanwhile, I have a meeting in

Frankfort with Mr. Leyre to read Dad's will. As you know, I'm the executor. Mr. Leyre said that it's a straightforward process. The house will go through Probate and all that.

Time to go to work. Be well and win this war for us soon, please. Carrie and the girls send their love, too.

Frank.

"Are you well, Jason?" Marcus took his cup and tipped more whiskey into it.

"My parents died back in September."

"Bloody hell! Both of them?"

Jason nodded. "Mom fell, then died in the hospital. She wasn't well already, and the fall did her in. Dad was heartbroken, I guess. It seems he had a heart attack driving back home from the hospital."

Moving to Jason's cot, Marcus sat down and put his arm around the devastated man's shoulder.

"I am so sorry for you, mate." They sat there while the shadows lengthened outside, gently sipping the single-malt Scotch. When the last sip was taken, Jason turned to his friend and broke down. Marcus held him tight while the tears from the new orphan dampened his shirt.

After a while, Jason stopped sobbing. He sat up and took a deep breath. "Sorry about that, Marcus."

"What's to be sorry about? If you hadn't cried, there'd have to be something wrong with you."

"Thanks, friend."

"I'm glad I could be here." Marcus looked at the remaining letter. "I'm afraid to mention it, but you still have another letter there."

"Oh, yeah." Opening the last letter, Jason read.

Independence, Missouri
October 20, 1942

Dear Jace,

Where do I begin? We're all here in Independence, in a new house close to the Lake City Army Ammunition Plant. It's an Army facility, but Remington runs it for them, and old 4-Fs like me are cranking out several different types of small arms ammunition. I'm in the R&D unit, testing new rounds for various Allied rifles and machine guns.

Dad's will confirmed that I was the sole heir. This was not a surprise; we all knew that Dad was passing the house and the rest to me. There wasn't anything except the house. The surprise was finding out that we couldn't keep it. The company decided that I should go to Independence, and the house is way too big for us to maintain. Besides, Carrie's parents live just outside Kansas City, so it was not a hard choice to sell the old house in Ilion and move here. The girls still have grandparents around. It's good here, and we can heal our wounds and replace the memories with new ones.

We packed all your things carefully in boxes, and we have a room for you here when you return to the States. If you settle somewhere else, we'll ship the boxes to you. We were careful not to make any choices for you; if we weren't positive it was ours, it's in your boxes.

The address here is RFD #32, Independence, Missouri. We're on a country road close to Buckner. The phone exchange is Independence 223.

Please come home safe. There's enough grief to go around in this war.

Carrie and the girls send their love. So do Doris and Jim (Carrie's parents, in case you forgot).

Frank

"Well? More bad news?" Marcus had moved back to his own cot.

Jason was silent as he digested the meaning of this latest letter. He felt anguish losing his parents and the home he grew up in, all in a single afternoon of his life.

At the same time, he knew that the home had never been his – or Frank's for that matter. He had left home once already when he went to Cornell for college; now the home had left him. Simple.

Only time would heal the loss he was feeling now for his parents. When his throat started to close, he put that thought down.

"Yes and no. On one hand, I'm not just an orphan; I'm a homeless orphan. My brother had to sell the house when he was sent to Missouri to another ammunition plant. On the other hand, it's near my sister-in-law's family, so they are settling in well and my nieces still have grandparents in their lives."

"You never got your own place, did you?"

"No. In a way, this is best. When this damn war is over, I can look out with no commitment to anywhere in particular. I can also get over the grief better by not walking around Ilion with its memories."

"You'll be fine." Marcus stoppered the bottle and put it in his duffel. "Fancy some of that French cuisine in the mess tent?"

Richmond

JASON LOCKHART paused on the step of the train, but he saw no one familiar on the platform. Not that he expected to recognize anyone. The letter from Nelson Smathers, the Chairman of Clinical Research, had said only that someone would meet him.

He pulled his duffel bag close and stepped down. At the other side of the platform, he put down the bag and looked around. Everyone seemed to know where they were going. Most of the men were in uniform, as he had been until just last month. He stopped a porter.

"Excuse me, where are the taxis?"

"Through that door and straight across, sir. That'll be Main Street. There's a stand there."

"Thanks." He shouldered his duffel and joined the crowd heading for the main exit. Out on the sidewalk, he queued up at the taxi stand.

"Doctor Lockhart, I presume?"

He turned to see a tall, slender woman with shining auburn hair and bright hazel eyes holding a sign with the word "Lockhart." She smiled and arched an eyebrow as if expecting a response to her corny cue. But Jason was flummoxed.

"Uh, yes. How did you guess?"

"Apart from the fact that you look like a lost Yankee?" She smiled. Her tone put him at ease, making him chuckle. "Over there." She pointed to a dark green Hudson parked on the other side of the street.

At the car, she opened the trunk. "Don't you have a footlocker or something at baggage claim?"

"No, this is it, Miss –?"

"Ardwood. Nancy Ardwood."

"I'm Jason."

"Not yet, you're not." She smiled at his surprise. "I'm still a student."

"But I don't mind. You're not my patient or my student."

"My Daddy taught me better than that. I'll call you Doctor Lockhart at least for today. Jump in—no, the other side." She slid smoothly into the driver's seat while he stumbled around to the passenger's side.

"Sorry, force of habit."

"I understand, but no one drives this baby but me. I almost have it paid off."

"Where are we going?"

"Unless you need the men's room in a hurry or are starving, we're going to your quarters. We could have walked, but I expected you to have more luggage."

"My brother has my things in Missouri. I'll send for them after I get settled."

"I heard that you were from New York."

"Before the war, yes. But our parents died, and my brother sold the house. So here I am with just a duffel bag."

"Sorry about your parents."

"Thank you. I'm dealing with it."

"Here we are." She pulled up in front of an antebellum house next to the Valentine Museum. "The College has contracts with boarding houses in the neighborhood. The Dean told me to settle you with Mrs. Crawford."

"This *is* close. And convenient. I expected to stay in a hotel and find a room while I looked for a home."

"You'll probably still want to find your own place, but this way, the College can put you to work sooner."

He followed her up the stairs. A thin woman in black, with silver hair drawn into a bun, welcomed them in. She eyed Nancy sternly.

"I know, Mrs. Crawford. I'll be on my way now." She turned to Jason. "The Dean would like to see you at two, so you have time to freshen up and change. I'll be back at one-thirty." She let herself out.

"I'm delighted to meet you, Doctor Lockhart." Mrs. Crawford led him upstairs. "You have a suite at the end of the hall. A small study, bedroom and its own water closet. The bath is in there." She waved at a door halfway down the hall.

Jason was still distracted. "Miss Ardwood seemed in a hurry to leave. I hope I haven't offended her."

"Heavens, no. She is a fine young lady, and she knows the rules." Seeing his confusion, she added. "No mixing of the sexes in the house. That's what the front porch is for."

"I see." He set his duffel on the floor in the study. It was small but well appointed: a desk, a reading chair with a floor lamp, bookshelves. He could see a comfortable-looking full bed and an armoire through the open bedroom door. "This is very nice."

"I hope you like it here, Doctor Lockhart. Starting tomorrow, you may take your breakfast and supper downstairs, but please give me a day's notice so that we cook enough for you."

"I will. Thanks." Giving him the room key, she closed the door behind her.

At one-thirty, Jason was standing on the porch as Nancy walked around the corner to his right. He admired her purposeful stride and her athletic grace. *This is no shrinking violet,* he thought. He liked that.

"Hello, Doctor, are you ready for a short tour on the way?"

"Sure." Seeing that she didn't slow down or stop, he took the steps two at a time to catch up with her.

"Are you always in a hurry?"

"Not at all, but I like to keep moving. I usually practice at this hour, and my body expects it."

"Tennis? I saw the gym bag and racket in the trunk."

"Uh-huh."

"I play tennis. Where?"

"There are several clubs in the city. I like the one at the University of Richmond because it's near my home."

"Would you like to play me?"

She turned to give him a long look up and down. "Why not?"

"Are the courts nearby?"

"Not UR, but the MCV courts are just at the end of this street." Medical College of Virginia.

"Could we play today? I've been on the train for two days. I have my racket."

"Sure." Her smile had a mischievous twist to it, but he thought it was cute.

She led him to the Egyptian Building, which housed the Medical College of Virginia and turned him over to the Dean's secretary.

***

"God, you're fast!"

"Game set and match, Doctor." Nancy stood easily by the net, relaxed and barely glowing from the exercise. Jason was soaked in sweat and breathing hard, but he was also high on endorphins.

"Do we have time for another game?"

"I won't let you win it, but you could try for a draw." She cocked her head and dared him with a smile.

"I may be out of shape after tromping around the desert for two years, but I'll get my game back. Let's do it."

She danced through the next half-hour, allowing a draw. Jason thoroughly enjoyed her sassy humor and her company. He felt no shame that she could beat him.

"Why do you look like a cat playing with its food?" He said as he caught his breath. She laughed.

"Because you looked so cocky when you asked me to play this afternoon."

"I concede that you are the best player I've ever met but give me some time."

"Considering that you haven't been able to play during the war, you're actually doing quite well. I wouldn't mind helping you with your recovery."

"Won't I drag your game down?"

"I still have the team that practices at UR. I'll stay in shape."

"Let's discuss the details over dinner. I have to eat out the first night anyway. Are you free?"

"Why, Doctor Lockhart, we only just met!" She tilted her head and batted her eyelashes. He laughed. She poked him in the chest. "I'll meet you at six." She headed for the ladies' locker room, while he walked back to Mrs. Crawford's house.

***

The following Monday, Jason walked to the new clinical research laboratory on the other side of the campus. While being toured, briefed, examined, and evaluated, he met the other men and the one woman on the clinical research faculty. Almost all were recently discharged medical officers like himself. He had attended his first planning meetings and met the staff in the lab.

Over the next few weeks, he settled into a routine of planning and coordinating trials, meeting with patients and other faculty, and on weekends, looking for an apartment. With the GI's returning from the war, housing construction had turned the suburbs into boom towns; finished places were hard to come by.

Three times a week, he met Nancy at the MCV tennis courts. She described herself as an army brat, so she had moved around a lot growing up. Upon his questioning, she admitted that she spent the war in Montréal, where she studied at McGill University. Although she obviously enjoyed his company and ribbing him, she kept the conversations short.

But she couldn't keep out of his mind. From his colleagues and the staff, he found out that the "team that practices at UR" was the American Lawn Tennis Association club. They told him that Nancy worked as a pro with both men and women. *That explains the car and graduate school tuition,* he thought.

"I can tell you don't read the sports section," said Mike Clancy, his principal lab technician. "Nancy Ardwood is going to put the Richmond club on the tennis map at the national championships next spring."

"In New York?"

"That's the one."

He also learned that she was in the first cohort of MCV's new PhD program in pharmacology. Classes and student labs were in the older buildings, so he never saw her off the court.

Not that he could obsess about the woman who haunted his dreams. His days were crammed with the busyness of building a brand-new research operation as the city around him madly raced to rebuild a peacetime existence. These were heady times for the surgeon-turned-researcher.

Still, in quiet moments, he would find himself grinning privately as he pictured those bright eyes laughing at him over her tennis racket or that smile that told him that she was happy to be there too.

***

After the fall break, Nelson Smathers called him to the department office. Elaine Johnson, the chairman's secretary, motioned him into the conference room off the reception area. There he found Dean Haag, Nelson, and the Chair of the Department of Pharmacology, whom

Jason had met early in the semester. *Gersheim*, Jason thought. *Ari Gersheim.*

"That's everyone," said the Dean. "Nelson?"

"Gentlemen, you know that the pharmacology program is very special at MCV, partly because it's our first academic degree program. We've had a proposal from one of the PhD candidates to carry out drug trials at our clinical research facilities."

"We're quite excited about it," said Professor Gersheim. "This student designed a program for us to do independent testing of new drugs for the local pharmaceutical companies. MCV has the newest facilities available anywhere, but we can't finance large scale trials on the meager grants the NIH sends us. The student approached Abbott, Pfizer and Smithson. They are willing to finance the trials – including indirect cost recoveries, of course."

"Now that the war is over," Jason said, "the government is pulling back research and development funding. I wondered when someone would notice." The others nodded.

The dean looked at Jason. "You have the labs, the companies have the money, and both they and the pharmacology school need the research."

"It sounds like a win-win to me," Jason said. "What do you need from me?"

Nelson answered. "When the time comes, the students will join our staff in the lab for the duration of the trials to which they are assigned. We'll set them up with internships. If you are willing to work with them, Doctor Gersheim here will ask one of us to sit on the dissertation committees of the PhD candidates that are participating. That's just one now. Except for that and the extra activity, it should be business as usual for us."

Jason left the meeting looking forward to new project. It would be more work, but he was busy already. He was excited to have younger people challenging the old timers. He had seen what teenagers and young adults could do in combat and in sandstorms; he missed them.

***

As the leaves turned and fell, Jason found a furnished apartment in the block between Mrs. Crawford's house and the MCV tennis courts. He felt his muscles returning to the form he had developed at Cornell before the war. Some of the faculty at the lab also played, so he was able to fit easier workouts in between the sessions with Nancy.

The week before Thanksgiving, he finally won a match with Nancy. In the time it took to walk to the net, they both recovered their breath.

"Thanks," he said.

"What for?"

"Letting me win at last."

"Jason, you won that fair and square. Congratulations."

"It's 'Jason' now?"

She grinned. "After our second game last summer, I decided when I would use your name."

"This feels like a graduation ceremony. Let me take us somewhere to celebrate."

"Not tonight, sorry." She chuckled at his crestfallen expression. "I need to be in top form tomorrow morning. Let's go out tomorrow night. By then, I'll have my dissertation proposal defended and be ready to relax."

"I forget that you're a student here when we're playing. What's it about?"

"Tell you tomorrow. Until then, only my proposal committee can ask that." She smiled and poked him with her racket. "If they accept the answer, I'd like to go to the Jefferson for dinner. Can you handle that?"

"I think so. I've been too busy to spend my severance pay from the Navy." She laughed.

"I don't eat that much, and we can go Dutch."

"I wouldn't hear of it."

"Okay. But don't be too proud with me. In case you haven't noticed, I like to carry my own weight."

"I noticed, and I'll remember to ask when I need to. Promise."

"I'll come by with the car about six. If it's nice, we can walk."

"See you at six, then. I'll make the reservations."

***

The next day, Jason moved through his duties in a distracted state. He did not know what Nancy was studying or where the dissertation proposal defense would be held, but he had no doubt that she would pass. There was nothing about that woman that accepted failure, he could tell.

Elaine Johnson called him in the lab just as he was about to go to lunch.

"A Miss Ardwood called for you."

"Nancy."

"Yes. She said that she would meet you as agreed."

"Did she leave a number?"

"No, sir."

"No problem. Thanks."

Back in the lab, he tried to concentrate on the pile of release forms on his desk. His principal lab tech walked in.

"You okay?" Mike asked. "You seem out in space today."

"Oh, I'm fine. To tell the truth, I have a date tonight, and it occurred to me that it's my first date since before the war."

"That explains it." Mike picked up the finished pile of forms. "I'll take these to Doris. You want to skip the calibration of the spectrometer today? It'll still be here Monday."

"Sure. It's close enough to quitting time. Let's call it a day."

***

Jason admired the skill with which Nancy backed the Hudson into the parking space outside his apartment building. He had stood in the space to keep it free after his neighbor had pulled out.

"It doesn't look like rain to me," she said. "But you're the sailor. Shall we walk?"

"I was a surgeon, not a sailor, but yes, let's walk."

She locked the car and took his arm. He enjoyed the pleasant warmth running up his arm like an IV drip of something strong. Standing almost as tall as he, she matched his stride in her low heels.

The Jefferson Hotel was a landmark of downtown Richmond, and the restaurant was arguably the finest in town. With rationing lifted, the staff had wasted no time in filling out the menu with the many delicacies that had established its renown before the war.

When they turned their coats over to the coat check attendant, Jason could appreciate Nancy's style off the court.

"Are you all right, Jason?"

He shook his head. "Sorry. I'm fine. And so are you, I confess. I've never seen you dressed for the evening."

"You look pretty good yourself." She took his arm as they approached the maître d'hôtel.

Over supper, Nancy asked Jason about his family, especially his twin nieces. Jason did not forget her promise.

"So, I take it you disarmed the defense, and they approved your proposal." She nodded. "Now you can tell me what it's about."

"But wouldn't that be talking shop? Bad manners, at least." She wiggled her eyebrows and left one in an inquiring arch. Jason chuckled.

"You are a very private person, but I can go to the Provost's Office and get a copy of the whole proposal, you know."

"Maybe I should let you do that." She smiled and cut a small piece of the filet mignon. "Tell you what. If you want to talk shop, I'll let you go first. What do you think of the facilities at the Clinical Research Lab? Say, compared to Cornell or wherever you worked after that."

Through the main course and salad, she kept the conversation focused on Jason's work. Clearly, she knew the layout and the equipment. Over the crème brulée, he tried to turn the subject.

"I think you know more about my lab than I do. Why haven't I seen you in our building?"

"I worked in your lab before you got here."

"What are you working on now?"

"I'm on a team comparing different protocols for cost-effectiveness."

"Sounds like a business school project."

"It does, doesn't it? Maybe I should get an MBA after this. Anyway, we don't need to be in the lab to run the numbers at this point." She stifled a yawn, but it caused him to yawn too.

"Coffee?" He signaled for the server.

"No, thanks. The walk back should wake us up." He asked for the check.

At the stairs to his building, they paused, each looking expectantly at the other.

"Mrs. Crawford doesn't live here, and I've known you for almost six months now," he said. "Would you like to come up?"

"Yes. I thought you were never going to get your own place." As they climbed the stairs, she slipped her arm in his and gave him an affectionate tug....

***

Jason awoke to the sun streaming in the east window. He opened his eyes and saw the familiar outline of the College beyond the trees across the street.

Then he smelled coffee. He leaped out of bed and ran to the bathroom for a robe. It was missing. *Nancy!* He jumped into the trousers that he had left on the chair and went to the kitchen.

"Good morning, sleepyhead. I don't know if you like the full American breakfast or the Continental, so I've only brewed coffee. She pointed to a chair and set a steaming cup down. "The milk went bad, so the coffee is black today."

"My fault. I don't use the milk fast enough." He sipped the coffee and looked at the beautiful woman sitting at his kitchen table. She was staring back, with that mischievous smile he had come to love. "What?"

"Just thinking about how smooth your skin is. I like that."

"Compared to what?" He blushed and looked down.

"Nothing in particular. I didn't know what to expect, and that stood out among my impressions."

"Thank you."

"For what?"

"For everything. Letting me celebrate with you. The tennis lessons. Getting to know you. Everything."

"Thank you, too." She rose. "So, breakfast?"

"What do you usually have?"

"Crusty bread or a croissant, jam, and café au lait. What about you?"

"The chefs in the mess tent were French. Pretty much the same." He took a loaf of French bread from the bread box, while she found the jam and butter in the refrigerator….

***

The weekend passed in a fog for Jason. Mostly he daydreamed of Nancy after she left Saturday morning. He was surprised to find out that she lived alone on the West End but had boarders. They were packing out, and Nancy would be inspecting their rooms on Sunday.

Monday morning, he was up early, feeling some anticipation for the week ahead. Ari Gersheim would come to introduce the Principal Investigator. The first cohort of student interns for new drug trials for Smithson Pharmaceuticals would arrive on Wednesday for orientation.

Smithson had only signed off on the arrangement on Friday, so the details had been kept confidential. Jason knew that drug companies were more secretive than the War Department when it came to new products, but he still felt a little annoyed to know so little two days before the start.

Elaine Johnson stepped into the lab as he was hanging up his coat.

"The Dean called for Doctor Gersheim, so he's sending the PI over alone."

"Still nine o'clock?"

"Yes. I'll bring her down."

"Her?"

"Yes, doctor." She crossed her arms and arched an eyebrow. "We're not all secretaries around here." Jason blushed with embarrassment.

"I'm sorry. With Madeleine on my team, I should know better." Madeleine had landed at Juno Beach in Normandy and followed the Canadian Expeditionary Force into France.

"Accepted." Elaine smiled. "One of the changes while you were gone. You'll get used to it." With a wink, she turned and left.

At nine, Elaine walked back in, with a familiar figure trailing her.

"Doctor Lockhart, this is Doctor Ardwood."

Jason stood and stared. "Doctor Ardwood? I thought you were a student."

"I am, but that didn't cancel my M.D."

Elaine was grinning. "I'll leave you two to get this rolling. Call me if you need anything." She left.

It took a minute for Jason to recover. He wanted to hug her and scream at the same time. Finally, he said. "Coffee, Doctor?"

She laughed. "Sure." She slipped out of her coat and hung it next to his. They walked down the hall to the break room "You can call me Nancy, unless you run a stuffier lab than you did last week."

"We're on first names here. Even the principal lab tech is a PhD in physics."

"I know Mike. He's one of the reasons I wanted your lab to run this program. Not much can go wrong with him in charge of the equipment."

"You're the PI? I thought you only just defended your dissertation proposal."

"I am and I did." She took two mugs with one hand and decanted coffee into each. She replaced the carafe, then handed a mug to Jason. "Ari would have explained it had he been here this morning. A medical doctor can direct research, especially at MCV, where we don't have academic degrees yet."

"I get it. That's why Ari is your advisor for the PhD."

"Right. But I can be the PI for the research itself and apply for grants."

"Weird, but I'm delighted to get to know you better." They turned into his office.

"Friday wasn't enough?"

Jason blushed. "Of course, but you know damn well you've been stringing me along."

Touching his cheek with the back of her hand, she looked into his eyes and said "I'm sorry about that. It's part of my nature not to volunteer more about myself than I must. I didn't expect Friday night."

He looked at the door in case to be sure of some relative privacy. "I hope it won't be the last time. I don't think this qualifies as fraternizing with the students."

"I hope so, too. We're peers here: my project; your lab." She smiled. He smiled back. "Are you going away for Thanksgiving?"

"I had forgotten about it. No."

"Good. You are hereby invited to our house for the traditional feast."

"Our? I thought you lived alone."

"I do – until tomorrow night. I'll be meeting my parents at the station. Dad is taking leave between duty stations."

"I'd be delighted. Can I come out early to help?"

"No need. I've been getting this ready for months." She looked at the clock. "I'll fill you in better later. Let's get Mike and Madeleine in here."

"Not so fast. I think you owe me some explanation about the research before we call them."

"You haven't read the proposal?"

"Of course not. Everyone has been handling this tighter than the plans for the Normandy invasion."

"I'm sorry, Jason. I gave it to Nelson on Friday." She looked past his shoulder to the desk. "I think that's it on your in-box."

Turning around, Jason lifted the heavy manuscript and sighed. "I left early Friday, so I didn't know it was here."

"That explains why you were so surprised this morning. I thought you were stringing *me* along Friday night."

"I take it Mike knows all about this."

"No. But he worked with my earlier research, so he knows what to expect." She picked up the coffee mugs. "While you read the introduction and as much of the research methodology as you can, I'll get refills. Okay?"

Shaking his head to reestablish his focus, Jason opened the dissertation proposal. Nancy proposed to examine two new drug lines doubling the number of runs to see if a protocol with fewer steps could achieve the same results as the current setup in Jason's lab.

When she came back, he looked up and grinned. "You *could* get your MBA with this."

"Maybe that's why Smithson likes it. Their honchos can understand it." She set his mug down. "Did you read enough to call in the others?"

"Sure. I'm used to chasing the troops to the fight. I'll catch up."

***

Wednesday afternoon, Nancy and Jason helped Mike and Madeleine close the lab for the long weekend. As Nancy had expected, Mike's team of technicians had set everything up on Monday, so they were off to a good start in the first three days.

"Tomorrow, I'll pick you up about one," said Nancy as they collected their coats in his office. "Is that too early?" She gave him that mischievous smile he loved.

"Of course not, but I could make my own way out there. Certainly, I can find a taxi even on Thanksgiving."

"That would cost more than flying to Missouri to be with your brother. I'll pick you up."

"Okay. I can see that you like to drive."

"That, too."

"Your father must be a career regular. Is that right?"

"Oh, yes. Why?"

"You've never told me much about him except that he's Army and you lived in Europe before the war. Where was he during the war?"

"Pacific theater."

"Maybe I can ask him."

"You could, but be prepared to get just as much as I got. He doesn't talk about the war. Ever."

Jason's expression darkened. "I can understand that."

As they walked to the exit, she added, "Bring your tennis kit and plan to stay over. We have plenty of room, and I don't expect you to make a fool of yourself."

"If I make a fool of myself, what then?"

"I'll take you home, or maybe make you sleep in the backyard."

He gave her a one-armed hug. "I'll take that risk. See you at one."

***

Jason did not make a fool of himself, but Thursday, he lived in terror of tripping on himself. Nancy had told him that the house was her father's childhood home, with room for generations and siblings. He was not prepared for the stately antebellum home on Three Chopt Road, less than a mile from the UR tennis courts and the Richmond Country Club. As Nancy drove the Hudson around the driveway to the front of the house, her parents came out to the porch.

Even before he could make out their features, Jason understood where Nancy got her height and her good looks. Colonel Matthew Ardwood stood at least six foot four; Annabelle Dampierre Ardwood close to six feet. She looked like a blonde version of Nancy. But there was another quality, which Jason recognized from his travels in France and Morocco: a confident bearing that was utterly feminine and alluring while conveying great strength of character. These were women who would never look old in any sense of the word.

Nancy hugged her parents, then turned to introduce Jason. Her father's handshake was firm, and his smile was wide. "I am very delighted to meet you, Jason. I've heard more about you than anything else for the last two days. This is my wife, Annabelle."

"*Enchanté, madame.*" Jason bowed slightly as he took her hand. Annabelle smiled.

"*Je ne savais pas que vous parliez français, monsieur.*" I didn't know you spoke French. Annabelle Dampierre looked at her daughter. Nancy shrugged.

"*Pas d'occasion, Maman.*" It didn't come up. She took Jason's hand. "It's been tennis and work, so far."

"Perhaps this will be the first of many pleasant surprises, *non?*" She indicated the door and led them into the house.

"I'm afraid it's rather plain," said Colonel Ardwood. "With boarders living here, we stored almost all our personal things."

Even without the memorabilia, the house did not lack for comfort or elegance, in a simple, understated way. They gave Jason a tour of the ground floor and the yard out back. Then he went for his tennis bag. Nancy showed him his room upstairs.

"Mom and Dad are down there on the end. My room is the one across from yours. Bathroom there in the hall, just like Mrs. Crawford's."

"I'll be right at home, then." Jason smiled. He looked around. "You're managing all this by yourself? With school, tennis, and research?"

"It's not that hard. When my grandparents died, Dad kept the gardener, the cook, and the housekeeper. The rent from the boarders pays for them. Of course, they're home for the weekend. We're on our own for the Thanksgiving feast."

"May I help?"

"Of course. Dump your stuff, hang up your coat and jacket, and come downstairs." Moving into his arms, she gave him a long, lingering kiss, then slipped out the door, closing it behind her.

**

While Jason sat on a stool in the corner of the kitchen whisking egg whites into a meringue, he enjoyed listening to Nancy and her mother swapping stories of their adventures since Nancy left Montréal. *One advantage to serving in North Africa,* he thought. *I could never have followed their French before the war.* He had helped her father set the dinner table. The colonel then went to the train station to meet his sister, Mary. Gravel crunching in the driveway signaled their return.

If Norman Rockwell had lived in Virginia, he would have painted Thanksgiving dinner in the Ardwood home. The conversation lasted until midnight, over drinks in the dining room and then in the kitchen as everyone helped clean up.

The next morning, they walked to UR for tennis. The family prevailed on Jason to stay Saturday night, with the thin excuse that Nancy could take Aunt Mary to the train station and Jason home in one trip. Clearly, they enjoyed his company as much as he enjoyed theirs.

***

The semester ended in the middle of December, though the research trials would continue through the winter. The evening of the last day of school, Jason took Nancy to the Jefferson and proposed. She paused with that mischievous smile before saying "yes."

Nancy insisted on a small wedding, with only their colleagues from the College, the Lockharts from Missouri, and Mary from Washington. In January, before leaving for a new duty station in Kansas, Colonel Ardwood gave his daughter away. The last boarder finished out his lease while they enjoyed a brief honeymoon in Paris. Nancy and Jason settled into the big house on Three Chopt Road.

INCHON

LIEUTENANT MIKE NORWOOD CINCHED the chin strap under his helmet and checked the mirror over the tiny sink in his stateroom. He hoped that he did not look as terrified as he felt. *Nothing to it,* he said to his reflection, *just let them do their jobs.*

He stepped into the tiny passageway, took a right and opened the door. The steady pounding of the big naval guns, which had been thumping the bulkhead of his sea cabin, suddenly increased in volume and speed. He squared his shoulders and stepped through.

"Captain on the bridge!" the quartermaster shouted. Normally, every man would have snapped to attention and stopped whatever they were doing. In combat, they dispensed with such ceremony. Instead, Lieutenant (junior grade) Hale, the Officer of the Deck (OOD), called out. "Ahead slow, 090, sir." He dropped his binoculars and turned to the skipper. "Ready to beach on signal." He indicated the flagship, another Landing Ship Tank (LST) four ships to starboard.

Mike shook hands with the Marine Corps officer standing next to the OOD. "Good luck today, Lieutenant." Like Hale, First Lieutenant Parker was a mustang—a former enlisted man.

Mike considered himself blessed: all the officers in his wardroom had seen service in World War II, a rare roll of the dice. Sergeant Norwood had received his appointment to the Naval Academy while in Italy, which took him out of the war for a while. On VJ Day, he had been riding a troop train somewhere in Kansas, only a few months after his commissioning.

"Put us past the surf, and we'll make our own luck, sir." Parker saluted and went to join his men and their tanks.

Since stepping on to the bridge, Mike's gaze had taken in the faces of the men there and scanned the scene beyond the bulletproof glass of the bridge windows.

Inside, his team of teenagers seemed pale but focused, each with his mouth set and keeping themselves busy to quell their own fear. Except for Hale, this was their first battle. The whistling of sixteen-inch shells overhead followed by explosions on the beach did not inspire the patriotic appeal of a fireworks show back home.

Outside, Mike saw a chunk of the cliff to their left blow away and crash to the beach below, bringing down the three houses above it. Smoke rose from the town of Inchon, mostly evacuated the day before by a fleet of Japanese ferry boats (re-purposed landing craft) brought up to clear civilians from the site of the expected landing.

Mike had admired the skill and discipline of the Japanese civilian captains who had gathered on the flagship LST to hammer out a set of flag signals to communicate with the American LST squadron staff. Neither the Japanese nor the Americans spoke the other's language, but they had managed to bring thousands of non-combatants away before the cruisers and battleships began softening up the beachhead.

Mike moved to the starboard side but did not bother to get in the captain's chair. He stepped out to the bridge wing, where he could see the flagship's signal halyards and hear the bridge team at the same time. The cold wind of mid-September held the signal flags stiffly out, making them easy to read. *USS LST-973* was almost the last ship on the left wing of the line of landing ships.

Off his starboard quarter he could see the silhouettes of the bombardment ships and the flashes of their guns. Beyond them, the hospital ship *USS Haven* (AH-12) cruised slowly back and forth, a big white patch against the gray horizon.

Twenty minutes later, the shelling doubled in intensity, and rows of gaily colored flags climbed the flagship's mast. Each LST in the line repeated the signal, until all thirteen ships were flying the same signal.

"Stand by, Mr. Hale."

"Aye, aye, sir!"

The string of flags on the flagship disappeared as signalmen snapped them down. The signalman behind *973*'s bridge shouted "Execute!" as he snapped his string down.

Mike nodded to the OOD.

"Full speed ahead. Come left to 085. Bo's'n, prepare to beach!"

The boatswain pulled down the microphone to the 1MC public address system and blew the call for "attack and board" (left over from the sailing days) on his shrill pipe. Every heart on board beat faster knowing that they were driving at full speed to put the bow of their ship as far up the beach as possible. Soon they would be stuck in the sand and at their most vulnerable.

From the bridge wing, Mike watched his crew do what they had drilled for months to do without thinking. Black smoke bellowed from the two exhaust stacks as the big diesel engines raced to maximum speed.

Every man grabbed something to steady himself as the ship caught a large wave and rode it into the beach. Still, Mike leaned over the rail slightly at the sudden stop.

"Ahead slow. Steady as she goes!" Hale called out. The helmsman used his wheel to keep the ship pointed into the sand without sliding the stern one way or the other. The engines slowed to keep the bow up on the beach as the wave receded.

"Nicely done, Mr. Hale." Mike smiled. Hale nodded and kept his mouth taut, but his eyes smiled.

The bow ramp went down as soon as the ship steadied into position. The ramp fell onto dry sand, well above the water mark, exactly as they had wanted. While the tide continued to come in, the tanks and amphibious assault vehicles with their Marines raced onto the beach. The 50-caliber machine guns on either side of the ramp added their noise to the din, firing over the advancing tanks.

The enemy artillery gave up trying to lob their shells at the bombardment ships. Mike saw the splashes of their shells walk back toward the beach. He prayed that they could back off before the enemy finished spotting them.

"All ashore, sir" the sailor on the sound-powered phone to the battle circuit called out. Mike gestured to the boatswain's mate at the ramp, which began rising rapidly. He could feel the slight movement of the ship, which began to float, being relieved of her cargo and the attachment of the ramp to the beach.

"Back us out, Mr. Hale."

"Half speed astern! Steady as she goes!" The great diesels stopped while the engineers shifted the transmissions into reverse. The ship shuddered as the engines grabbed the propellers shafts. The helmsman's knuckles whitened over the wheel, ready to counteract any sideways swing of the stern.

Mike saw the LST two ships over from him take a direct hit just below the bridge. Shrapnel the size of a small car flew into the air, to land in the water and rain on the LST next door. A shell crashed into the water between *973* and the next LST backing out. *Too close,* he thought.

A pair of Marine Corsair fighter-bombers flew low overhead toward a gun emplacement on the cliff. The *burrpp* of their strafing rounds punctuated the thump of the heavier artillery on the beach in front him and the naval gun line behind him.

LST-973 gained speed as she pulled into the high tide. Hale increased speed and ordered the stern to port. Mike walked over to the port bridge wing, where he could see the other ships and the landing. Just as he stepped out, the world became silent; a blazing light surrounded him and went out…

***

Light. Everywhere. It had been dark, but now he could see light and hear sounds. Shadows appeared against the light.

Suddenly he felt a great pain throughout his body. Worse than burning, like the twisting of a hot knife in every muscle. As the shadows took shape, the pain grew greater in his left side and then his shoulder and chest. He gasped.

"Michael." A woman's voice. The shadow slowly became a brown-haired woman with dark eyes and a gentle smile.

Not Margery, he thought. She waved her hand. "Follow my hand, Michael." He did, and his head began to spin.

He tried to speak, but he was too tired. He closed his eyes…

He opened his eyes. A bright light blinded him, so he shut his eyes quickly. He felt more than saw a shadow block the light. He opened them again. A man in a white lab coat leaned over him. By the khaki uniform under the coat, Mike recognized a Navy surgeon.

"Hello, Lieutenant. I'm Doctor Lockhart. You're going to be OK." Mike tried to smile, but the effort hurt. "Easy now. There's no hurry. You just rest and let your body finish repairing itself."

Mike closed his eyes. Without the bright ceiling light in his face, he could smile. "Thanks," he said, and slept.

When he awoke next, he felt strangely refreshed. His left shoulder, arm and chest hurt terribly, but the rest of him felt almost normal. The brown-haired nurse caught his glance as she passed his bed. She came to his bedside.

"Hello, Mr. Norwood. How do you feel now?" She smiled and picked up his chart from the foot of his bed. He could not help noticing how well her khaki uniform fit.

"Hurts like hell."

"Welcome back to the living, then. The pain will get better."

"Where am I? What happened?"

"*USS Haven*. We're off Inchon now, but we could be heading south any time – or tying up if the troops advance inland."

"My ship?"

She checked the chart again. "*973* is still out there. I think Doctor Lockhart has more information for you. I'll send him around."

"Thank you, Lieutenant—" He squinted to see her name badge.

"Phillips." She held a glass of water to his lips. He drank deeply, then fell back. "I'll be right back."

Doctor Lockhart came walking down the ward almost as soon as Lieutenant Phillips' shapely figure disappeared through the watertight door. He checked the chart, then took Mike's wrist to check his pulse.

"Strong. That's good. How's the pain?"

"Terrible, but it's not all over like before."

"That's good. I don't want to give you morphine unless you really need it."

"Can you fill me in on what happened? I don't remember anything."

"Nothing to remember. A mortar round hit your ship just below the bridge on the port side. The explosion sent a piece of steel into your left shoulder. The port lookout was knocked unconscious, and three men on the foredeck took shrapnel."

"How did I get here? What happened to the ship?"

"Your crew brought you to us in the whaleboat. The ship continues with the squadron, minus the port wing of the bridge."

"How long have I been out?"

"Almost two weeks now. You were in a coma for the first ten days, and we don't want to move you until you are ambulatory, if possible."

"So, what happens now?"

"You keep healing. When we see how well you're doing, we'll either return you to *973* or a transport for repatriation."

Two days later, Nurse Phillips and a corpsman helped Mike out of bed. He felt lightheaded, and his legs were weak after all the inactivity, but he walked to the end of the ward and back.

By the middle of October, he could walk up the ladder outside the ward and join the other officers in the wardroom between meals. Patients had to eat in their wards. The wardroom could only accommodate the ship's officers.

Doctor Lockhart sometimes joined him for cards or conversation.

"From what Nurse Phillips tells me, you saved my life, Jason," Mike said as he swept up the hand he had just won. The surgeon smiled and blushed modestly.

"Your crew saved your life, Mike. I just patched you up. If they had hesitated at all to get you to us, we'd have lost you. And it *was* close. It took us six hours to sew all the pieces together, but the real danger was in the time you spent unconscious, because we did not know what kind of damage your head sustained."

***

Mike Norwood returned to his ship. Lieutenant Hale handed him his helmet, which was caved in dramatically. "There's a new one in your cabin, sir."

The squadron commodore came aboard just before Christmas. He pinned a star on Mike's Purple Heart medal (in lieu of a second award), and medals on the rest of the crew. The ship herself received a Navy Meritorious Unit Commendation. Hale received an immediate promotion to full Lieutenant and orders to take command of a new LST in Yokosuka.

USS-973 remained off Korea with the United Nations counteroffensive until the following spring. A year after Inchon, Mike brought her alongside the pier in San Francisco. The ship became the Republic of France Ship (RFS) *Golo* and sailed back to the Western Pacific. Mike spent Christmas at home in San Diego with Margery.

And every Christmas, Jason Lockhart would receive a bottle of single-malt Scotch whisky, and a simple, unsigned card with one word.

"Thanks."

Jason's Last Wish

NANCY LOCKHART TAPPED THE HORN when she parked in the driveway. Adele came out to the porch. Joe ran around the housekeeper and threw his arms around Nancy's waist.

"Adele, could you help me get this stuff into the house? I stopped at the post office on the way home. I think it's Christmas packages." She leaned over and kissed her son. "You want to carry something too?"

"Yes. Is something for me?"

"I don't know. Nothing with your name on it. And if it's a Christmas present inside, we'll have to wait, won't we?"

Joe sighed and took the lightweight box she gave him. The two women loaded the other boxes and envelopes into the library. Joe checked each one, hoping to see his name. Then he returned to his room, where he was building something extraordinary with blocks, sticks, pieces from an Erector set, and folded cardboard sheets.

After she changed into a skirt and blouse, Nancy returned to open the packages. As she slit the first wrapping, she heard Jason's car pull up outside. She went to the porch. Flurries of snowflakes danced lightly in the streetlights, but a major storm was not expected.

"You're early. I only just got home myself." They walked into the house.

"Well, it's not for a good reason. The patient we were going to operate on this afternoon died this morning."

"That's terrible. I'm so sorry. Wasn't that just an appendix?"

"Yes, but there was something wrong with his immune system. He had symptoms of a simple cold last night. His organs began failing around midnight. He was dead by ten a.m. The family authorized an autopsy. I hope we can figure this out because it was a total surprise to us."

"Not a pathology or an infection?"

"Except for the cold, no."

"Take off the coat and tie and come relax. We had packages in the mail today. Some from Missouri." Jason's brother and his family lived near Independence.

Nancy met him with a glass of Riesling when he returned. He put it on the desk and embraced his wife. A long, lingering kiss put their busy world into its proper context.

"Thanks. I needed that."

"Me, too."

Armed with letter openers, they attacked the pile of packages. Nancy started a list for thank you letters in a notebook.

"This one looks like what we got last year and the year before. No return address."

"Any guesses?"

"I'd say it's a bottle of single malt whisky."

Opening the package, they saw a gift-wrapped box about the right size for a bottle of liquor. A blank card attached read simply, "Thanks."

"This is the third year. Do you have any idea who this is?" She set the gift under the tree with care, positioning it so that it would not break when it encountered an exuberant five-year-old on Christmas morning.

"Not really. It started after Inchon. I got the first one on board after we returned to San Francisco. This is the second one here in Richmond."

"Anyone especially grateful about Inchon?"

"So many. I was up to my elbows for days on end. They kept us off Inchon for months, using helos to bring the wounded out as they pushed inland."

She leaned over and kissed him. "Let's consider it a gift from all of them. From what I heard, you gathered quite a fan club from both wars."

"Wait a minute." Jason put his palms to his forehead and closed his eyes. "There was a lieutenant, the skipper of an LST during the landing itself. We played cards while he rehabbed on board. I sewed him together okay, but he was in a coma for two weeks, so we were not sure he would survive."

"He survived, I take it."

"Yes, and he returned to his ship." He opened his eyes. "Mike. Mike Norwood. LST-973. He said he owed me a bottle of Scotch every year for the rest of his life."

"The man keeps his word." She smiled. "I like that."

"Hi, Daddy!" a streak of red attacked Jason at knee level. "I didn't hear you."

"I didn't hear you, either. Are you up to something?"

"I built a space base, with a school and a hospital and an apartment building."

"Can I see it?"

"Not yet. I have to figure out how to build a bubble for it. There's no air in space, you know." He went to the stairs. "I'll call you when it's ready."

"Okay, son." Jason listened to the little feet scamper back up to their son's bedroom. "Space base?" He looked inquiringly at Joe's mother as he picked up the letter opener.

"I think my Aunt Mary had something to do with that. She spent a lot of time explaining what they are doing at NASA, where she works."

"National Aeronautics and Space Administration. Isn't that part of the Air Force?"

"Not really. It's at Langley Air Force Base, but as a tenant."

"Just a few years ago, I could not imagine going into space. But the new jets have broken the sound barrier. It's just a matter of time."

"That's what she says."

With all the packages opened, and presents under the Christmas tree, they moved to the envelopes. About half for each of them.

***

Amelia Banner, Nancy's secretary, stood in the door to her office. "Doctor Lockhart? Your husband is on the phone. Shall I tell him to call back?"

Nancy put a pencil in the thick research grant proposal she was reading. "No, Amelia. I'll take it." *He never calls me at work.*

She picked up the handset and pushed the blinking button on the phone. "Hello, Jason. Is everything okay?"

"Everything was okay until I heard your voice. Now everything is wonderful." Nancy smiled and felt a blush of pleasure. After more than six years, he still amused her with his romantic silliness.

"My day is a little brighter, too, but you must have called about something else."

"Oh, yes. Something much less important than flirting with you. Remember Edouard Manérin?"

"The French Consul. Of course. Émilie is in Joe's pre-school class."

"He would like me to take a trip, but he wants to explain it to both of us, over lunch. Would you be free on Thursday?"

Nancy looked at her desk calendar. "Unless Amelia is out there scribbling something new, I'm free. Where?"

"The Jefferson at noon. He *is* French, so I would block two hours and not schedule any boring presentations in the afternoon."

Nancy laughed. "If he wants to do this at the Jefferson instead of his office, it's probably dangerous, illegal, or embarrassing. He must want you to say yes very badly."

"He does have my attention, although I have no idea what he wants."

"Let's do it. See you tonight." She smacked a kiss in the phone.

"I love you. Bye."

They hung up.

***

Jason and Nancy did not dine often at the Jefferson Hotel, but its dining room held special memories for them. They had come here to celebrate Nancy's dissertation proposal defense, and it was on a later dinner date that Jason had proposed. Occasionally, Smithson Pharmaceuticals took out-of-town investors and visiting executives to the Jefferson, so Nancy had seen more of it at lunchtime than Jason had.

Edouard Manérin was standing in the lobby when they arrived.

"Doctors Lockhart, a pleasure to see you both." The Consul spoke English with an American accent, having attended the American School in Paris before going to the prestigious School of Public Administration. He bent over Nancy's hand with a quick kiss and shook hands with Jason. "Émilie seems quite taken with Joe. She has not mentioned any other boys in the class."

"*Peut-être qu'ils ne se sont pas encore frappés,*" she said. Maybe they haven't hit each other yet.

Manérin laughed heartily. Jason said in French, "At five years old, it could mean anything or nothing, but I am glad that neither has come home complaining."

"Please," said the consul motioning to the door to the restaurant, "let's have our lunch."

Conversation for the first part of the meal revolved around the two families. Their two children were the only ones in the five-year-old class who could already read, so they found themselves sitting together, reading quietly while the teachers and aides worked with the other children. Joe had picked up some French from Nancy's conversations with her mother, and Émilie said that he had a Parisian accent.

Over the cheese, the Consul refilled their wine glasses and nodded to the waiter. The servers withdrew.

"You've heard the saying, 'we have been doing so much with so little, that we can do the impossible with nothing', haven't you?" Jason and Nancy nodded. "As you know, I served in Equatorial Africa after the war. We had a saying there, *donnez ça à Jace*." Give that to Jace. "The mythical man who could do anything with nothing."

After a stunned silence, Nancy asked, "Is this some kind of coincidence? Jace isn't a French name." It was her husband's nickname.

"No. One of my colleagues, who had spent the war in and around Casablanca, told me that the saying was brought to Ubangi-Shari by Free French veterans."

"Why are you telling us this?" asked Jason.

"Because we are trying to do the impossible again." He took a sip of his wine and gathered himself. "You know that the situation in Indochina is not going well."

"I read about the battle at Dien Bien Phu. Aren't there peace talks in Saigon now?"

"And Paris. But the point is that the war in Vietnam has exhausted our resources, which we needed for our other colonies. We are trying to carry on in places like Africa and the Pacific, but those places are restive also."

"What are you asking?"

"We would like you to join a team of American and Canadian medical personnel to help us set up a teaching hospital in Bangui."

"French Equatorial Africa."

"Yes. Bangui is the capital and the only major city in Ubangi-Shari. It is also the last town that can be reached by water north of Brazzaville. The city serves a vast area that includes Chad, inland Cameroon, and the northern half of the Middle Congo.

"If we can put a teaching hospital there, it would help lift the area toward self-sufficiency."

"Which would ease the pressure on the French resources."

"Yes. The consular corps throughout North America is recruiting people like you."

"Why me?"

"Because of the work you did in Fedhala and Algeria. The work you did at MCV. What you did off Korea. And what you do every day at Saint Mary's here in Richmond."

"It takes more than a surgeon to set up a teaching hospital. Are you asking us to move to Bangui?"

"No. Your role would be to review our plans and watch us get started. Specifically, we'd like your expertise as a surgeon. We have administrators, researchers, and teaching professors of most specialties already."

Jason looked at Edouard silently for a long time.

"You have more passion for this than simply carrying out orders, Edouard."

"It shows, doesn't it?" He smiled. "The other consuls are doing their jobs, assembling teams and forwarding recommendations, but I have a personal interest. I love the people in Bangui. And I am afraid that they are going to need surgeons very badly, very soon. I want this project to be there for them."

"More war?"

"Worse. You did not hear me say this, but Vietnam is the tip of iceberg. I predict that in four years, my country will withdraw from central Africa, and by the end of the decade, from the rest of the continent.

"Then the nightmare will begin."

Nancy said, "You could have pitched this in your office. Why lunch, and why me?"

"Because if you did not have Joe, I would be asking for you as a team. Your reputation at MCV and Smithson matches his. I want you both in on this offer."

"When and how long?" asked Jason.

"We think six months. The planning is done. The Health Service in Brazzaville and Bangui would start construction after the review team helps them fix anything you can see. We figure two months. Then four months to see the project started. That should be enough to see if the actual work will proceed as planned." He paused. "What do you think?"

"Do you have some of these plans?"

"I can send you the executive summaries and basic drawings for all the infrastructure, and the high-level planning documents for the medical school staffing and tentative curricula. Enough for you to see what the Health Service is trying to do and get an idea whether it is practical."

"Who is doing the work?"

"The Colonial Administration, but a major goal of the project is to bring in as much local manpower as possible. We want the local population to keep it going."

Jason and Nancy looked at each other.

"When do you need an answer?"

"Last week would be ideal, but let me know how long it will take you to look at the documents, and we'll adjust our plans accordingly."

"That seems fair," said Jason. "Will you forward the materials to Smithson or Saint Mary's?"

"To your home if you don't mind. The involvement of non-French personnel in the project is a sensitive issue. That is the other reason for meeting here instead of the Consulate."

"Understood. We'll let the housekeeper know to accept the documents for us."

They rose, shook hands, and walked to their respective afternoon commitments.

***

For four days, Nancy and Jason pored over the box of documents that Edouard had sent over. They took notes and discussed their impressions.

On the fourth evening, the dining room table was covered with plans, maps and typewritten reports. They had given little Joe a copy of *L'Histoire de Babar* to keep him from taking papers from the table. He read happily to himself (out loud) in the corner, as best he could, stopping to figure out the words from the pictures.

"Here's another weak link between Brazzaville and Bangui," said Nancy. "I see no discussion about how medicines get to the hospital from the free port in Brazzaville. Especially the ones that need refrigeration or special handling. Are the boats on the rivers equipped for that?"

"Good point. I think I've covered surgery and the emergency department as far as I can go." Jason stood back, stretched, and refilled their wine glasses. "Let's make one more pass, taking notes about what we don't see – like the pharmacy and childcare center."

"More than childcare. Relatives of urgent patients will need short-term accommodation, and they will need facilities for the families of the med students."

"Let's put him to bed first." Jason sat on his heels in front of their son. "*Es-tu prêt á te coucher, mon fils?*" Ready for bed, my son?

"Read me what *Grandmaman* wrote here." Joe handed the book to his mother as Jason carried him on his shoulder.

Nancy read the inscription from her mother, which Annabelle Ardwood had penned in a beautiful cursive when she gave the book to Joe for Christmas. Joe was asleep before they reached his room.

By midnight, Nancy and Jason had assembled thirty pages of notes in French to be typed by the Consulate. Twenty of those pages came from Nancy, whose expertise in management and organization exceeded her husband's. They had agreed to accept the proposal. Jason had more than enough vacation time backed up to qualify for a sabbatical.

***

Jason stepped through the door of the jetliner and almost fell backwards from the weight of the hot air pressing against him. A layer of shining dew immediately covered his suit and exposed skin as the humidity condensed on his still-cool person.

Except for the initial sense of drowning for one breath, the warmth felt good. As he made his way down the ladder, he started sweating underneath his clothes.

He had been flying for four days: first from Washington to Montréal on a Colonial Airlines DC-4. There, the team of

Canadians, mostly from Québec, joined him on a Comet operated by the British Overseas Airways Corporation to London. The next day, they boarded the weekly BOAC jetliner to Paris, Nice, Algiers, Casablanca, and Brazzaville on its way to Cape Town.

Two days later, the team boarded riverboats for the long trip up the Congo and Ubangi Rivers. It took another six days to reach their destination. Jason's head sometimes hurt from weeks of working in French. Unlike Nancy, who had learned the language growing up, Jason had studied it in school and gained fluency during the war in Francophone Africa. It was an acquired skill, not a natural one.

"Mind a little company in English?" Jason started slightly as Leo MacDermott leaned on the railing next to him. Big-shouldered and medium height, the Scottish-Canadian epidemiologist smiled and reached into his pockets for his pipe and tobacco.

"Is it that obvious?"

"No, but sometimes I wear out by the end of the day – and I grew up in Québec."

"Thanks. I feel better."

They scanned the riverbank in silence for a few yards, as the boat pushed against the current.

"Beautiful, isn't it?" said Jason.

"Aye, and as unspoiled a piece of earth as you'll ever see. I hope we're not ruining it with our so-called civilization." He took a long puff and turned to Jason. "Good work, by the way. I came on board at the last minute, and the stuff you contributed on epidemiology and research facilities was spot-on. Couldn't have done better myself."

"My wife Nancy came up with all that." To his look of surprise, he added. "She's Head of Research at Smithson. She noticed that this hospital would be a perfect place for field studies."

"She's right. There are diseases in that jungle that we have never heard of."

***

There are only two seasons near the equator. Ubangi-Shari enjoyed a short dry season from December to February. By paying attention and sleeping under mosquito netting, the North Americans avoided sunburn, heat exhaustion, and malaria.

The Health Service had done a good job of quickly adjusting the plans, so that when site work began in March, things looked good on the ground. They had chosen a site on the edge of the jungle, two miles from the river. Jason could imagine the neighborhood growing around the hospital, especially with the potential for a university just southeast of the site. Expansion plans included a pediatric unit.

By June, the rough site work showed where the facilities would be. Most of the fine-tuning had to do with the logistics of moving materials up the river; the design and the construction plan was sound. The advisors were looking forward to returning home at the end of the month.

On the fifteenth, Jason was looking at some plans for the nurses' barracks when he heard shouting from the work site across the street. He knew the sound of an injured man instinctively. Grabbing the medical bag that he never let out of his sight, he ran toward the commotion.

One of the laborers guiding a steel beam held by a backhoe had slipped and fallen. The beam had swung and come out of its sling. It smashed the man's arm and bounced away.

Jason raced to the man while the backhoe operator lowered the end of the beam away from the scene. The man should not die from a crushed arm, but Jason recognized a man falling into shock. He was screaming in Sangho. Jason recognized *docteur*, but the man kept pushing him away.

The backhoe operator knelt next to Jason and said to him in French.

"He says he does not want a doctor. He is afraid of your medicine."

"Is there someone he would trust?"

"His medicine man. The tribe lives just over there." He motioned to the north with his head.

Jason could tell that the man would soon faint. "Please ask him in Sangho if I could treat him enough to take him to his *docteur*."

The backhoe operator asked the wounded man in Sangho. That Jason was offering to transport him to his people seemed to calm him. He nodded. "*Singila.*" Thank you. And he fainted.

Jason bandaged the wounds and splinted the arm. They loaded the man into a jeep that a relative working on a nearby site brought over. They allowed Jason to ride with them into the jungle north of the newly dug earthworks. The injured worker woke up on the way.

Along the way, Jason scratched an itchy scab on his arm. The worker's blood was still on his forearms, but Jason had often worked with blood up to his elbows and thought nothing of it.

A half-hour later, the road ended. The men in the jeep got out and helped their relative to his feet on the ground. He wobbled but insisted on walking with the others. Dozens of silent men and women appeared out of the forest as they walked. They reached a clearing not ten yards across. A solitary hut stood among the trees at the edge.

A man watched them from the entrance to the hut. Somewhere between middle-aged and old, Jason thought he looked too fit for the whiteness of his hair and the lines in his face. Jason followed the trio approaching the elder but kept silent.

The elder told them to sit. Jason knew that much Sangho. When the four men were seated cross-legged around him, the elder examined the arm and looked into the eyes of the wounded man.

"Your bandage, European?" he asked Jason in French.

"Only enough to get him here safely, *wanganga*." The elder arched an eyebrow at Jason's use of the Sangho word for doctor.

"No drugs? No potions?"

"No. He only needs his arm set. You or I can do that."

"You are an unusual European."

"I will take that as a compliment, *wanganga*."

"It is. Let us do this together." He ordered the men to bring out the chair inside the hut. Together, the two medical men undid the bandage and reset the bone. The worker used a piece of leather to bite down on, but otherwise bore the pain silently.

The elder let Jason clean the wound with antiseptic from his bag and sew up the gash. When that was done, the elder brought out a paste in a bowl and smeared it on the wound.

"May I ask what that is?"

"A salve. You would call it an antibiotic, but we have been using it for centuries to speed healing."

"May I take some? My woman is a healer, expert in our medicines. She would be delighted to study this."

The elder spooned some of the salve into a small jar from Jason's bag. "A gift. Thank you for caring for our cousin."

The jeep driver took Jason back to town.

The laborer was back in two days. The cut had closed over and was healing without infection. Jason asked about the stitches, and the worker said that the *wanganga* told him to leave them until the weekend, that he would remove them.

***

"Daddeee!" With a squeal of delight, Joe grabbed Jason around the waist. His father almost tripped from the impact. He bent over his son and drew Nancy to him with his free arm. Joe put his arms around them both while they kissed.

The family walked to the end of the platform of the Broad Street station and out to the parking lot. Twenty minutes later they were home. It was well after Joe's bedtime, so they attended to that first. Then Nancy and Jason could make up for lost time....

***

A week later, Nancy woke from a deep sleep. Jason was burning hot and sweating. The clock on the nightstand showed three a.m. She eased out on her side and came back from the bathroom with some aspirin and a thermometer. Jason was awake.

"My God, Jason. One hundred one." Nancy gave him the aspirin and a glass of water. What do you feel, dear?"

"Like I have a cold, except that it's just the fever. Aches but no runny nose – yet."

At dawn, his fever was 102°F. Nancy got Adele up and asked her to see Joe to day school. She drove Jason to Saint Mary's, then came back to get ready to go to the office.

At eleven o'clock, Amelia announced a call from Saint Mary's.

"Nancy, it's Mel." Melvin Schroeder was an internist and an endocrinologist. He was on a first-name basis with all the known germs and parasites in the human blood stream. Jason, Nancy, and Mel had been researchers together at MCV after the war.

"Is this about Jason?"

"Yes. Could you come here? It's complicated on the phone."

"Twenty minutes." She hung up.

"Amelia. I'm going to Saint Mary's. I don't have any appointments this afternoon, do I?"

"No. You wanted to go over the office budget, but that only involves you and me."

"Let's do it later. I don't know what this is about, and I don't know when I'll be back."

"Give my best to Jason, and don't worry. We have your back here."

"Thanks."

***

Melvin pointed to the settee in his office. Nancy sat. He drew up a chair.

"We're baffled, Nancy. Here." He took some lab reports from his desk and passed them to her. "His immune system is going nuts. We give him antibiotics for the infection, but his blood seems to eat the stuff. And he has almost no antibodies, not even for the things he was vaccinated for: smallpox, rubella, etc."

Nancy read the figures from the lab. "Is this like that patient with a cold back before Christmas? Jason described something like this."

"Yes. Shall we go see Jason?"

They walked to the ward together. Jason was sitting up, reading a newspaper. Nancy went to him and kissed him.

"Has Mel explained this to you?" she asked.

"Not that there is much to explain, eh, Mel?"

The three doctors looked at each other in silence. Nancy took a sharp breath.

"What happened to your arm?" The IV site on Jason arm had a bruise spreading halfway around his elbow.

"I don't know. The injection was unremarkable, but that's one hell of a bruise. All since this morning."

"We'd better stop the aspirin," said Mel, "before that turns into something worse than a bruise."

"What else do you feel, dear?"

"Nothing really, just tired. The fever is down, although that may be a reaction to the aspirin."

"Good enough to go home?"

"That's up to Mel here, but if nothing is going to change here, I might as well."

Mel said, "Let's take out the IV. You're eating and drinking normally. If nothing changes overnight, we'll discharge you in the morning."

"I'll bring little Joe back before supper." Nancy kissed her husband.

"Thanks. I'd like that."

***

A week later, Jason was back in the hospital with pneumonia. While there, he started losing weight, no matter how much they fed him. By September, he had lost forty pounds and was bedridden most of the time. Melvin noticed a virus on a blood test that he did not recognize, and he thought he had seen them all. The lab photographed the slides of Jason's blood samples and sent them to the National Institutes of Health.

Every day, Nancy and Joe visited him in the hospital. Jason and Joe read stories to each other.

On Thanksgiving, he went into the hospital for the last time. His body was breaking down, eating itself from the inside. Dr. Lambert, Joe's pediatrician, advised against having Joe near his dying father so much, but Joe sensed that his father wanted him there. Joe had never seen anyone die before, so he approached each day with his father as another day for them to enjoy.

Nancy understood this. She took Joe in every day.

Pearl Harbor Day was a Tuesday that year. After school, Nancy drove Joe to Saint Mary's, where Jason was in palliative care.

Jason sat up in the bed, his face pale, the skin pulled taut over the bones of his face.

"Hi, Daddy." Joe sat up on the bed. By now there was plenty of room for him next to his father's shriveled body.

"Hi, Joe."

"You're yellow today."

"It's called jaundice. My liver has failed, son."

"That's bad, right?"

"It just is, son. We knew this day would come, didn't we?"

Joe nodded solemnly.

For the first time since Jason first fell ill last summer, Joe and his father cried. Silently. Nancy let her tears fall and knelt by the bed, one hand on each of her men. She saw the pulses on the monitor next to the bed get lower and lower.

"I know you two will take care of each other. Am I right?"

"Yes, Daddy."

"Yes, dear."

"Kiss me, lover. Hug me, son."

They did as he asked. When they pulled back, Jason smiled and sighed.

"Thank you. I love you both." And he closed his eyes.

Nancy put her arms around her son. Joe hugged her back.

The monitor squealed as the trace flatlined.

Last Respects

"ALVIN! THAT'S CRAZY!" Thelma Monroe collapsed in a kitchen chair and put her head in her hands. Her proud, beautiful frame seemed to shrink in terror.

Her husband pulled a chair next to her and hugged her.

"Darling. That man is the reason I am here today, and that Tony has a father!"

"I know, but—" she circled the bottom of the obituary with her finger. "That's a white church in the West End. They won't let you in."

"I have to try. And I have an idea."

"What?"

"I'm going down to Chuck's Canteen to put the word out. Cookie will see that the right men come with me."

"Your pals from the war? What good would that do?"

"Trust me, Thelma. Some blood is thicker than hatred. Trust me."

"Oh, Alvin. Please don't come back from the war just to die at home."

"I won't, dearest. I won't."

***

"Hello?"

"Commander Norwood, sir. It's Peter Hale."

"Pete! Good to hear from you. Where are you?"

"Norfolk, sir."

"Pete, call me Mike. We're both commanders now. I hope you're not paying for this call. I'm on the West Coast."

"Thanks, Mike, and, yes, I am. I think it's important."

"Well?"

"Jason Lockhart died. It was in the obituaries in the *Virginian-Pilot* this morning."

"When is the funeral?" Pete told him. They rang off quickly. Long-distance phone calls could dent even a Navy commander's budget.

Mike Norwood went to the kitchen. Margery was just starting breakfast…

***

"It's General Puller, sir." The lieutenant answering the phone spoke in hushed tones, never having ever expected in his life to hear the voice of the living legend.

His boss rose and picked up the receiver, unconsciously standing at attention.

***

In the Embassy of France on Reservoir Road in Georgetown, the direct line rang in the ambassador's office. The conversation was in French. The caller was the consul in Richmond, Virginia.

"Jason Lockhart has died. His funeral is next week."

"What happened?"

"No one knows. He turned ill a week after returning from the Congo."

"*Mon Dieu!* That was only six months ago. I never knew."

"I think I should attend. He—"

"Georges, give my secretary the details. And order a floral arrangement from the Republic of France. I will drive down Friday."

"Very well, Excellency. Please be our guest."

***

"Hello, sergeant, how are you?" Matthew Ardwood smiled as he approached the cash register in the diner across from the Broad Street Station.

The owner of the diner gaped, then stood at attention.

"Colonel Ardwood! What can I get you?" They shook hands and held the gesture until the urge to cry passed.

"How many of the 27th do you know around here?"

"I'd say maybe a half-dozen, sir. There's not many of us left, you know, but we meet at the VFW every month." Most of Matthew's unit was wiped out at the Battle of Guadalcanal.

Matthew saw the *Richmond Times* lying on the counter. "Have you checked the obituaries today?"

"Not yet, sir."

"My son-in-law is in there. Read between the lines, and you might want to join us at the funeral. And if there are any veterans of Operation Torch or Anzio at the VFW, you might want to let them know."

***

"Joe, you don't have to go. You can stay here with Mrs. Paterno."

Nancy hugged her six-year-old son for the third time since dawn, when they had both awoken from nightmares.

"No, Mommy. I want to go. I'll try not to cry."

Nancy knelt on one knee and took him by the shoulders. She held him out, so they were staring into each other's eyes. Tears ran down their cheeks.

"It's okay to cry. In fact, I don't want you to hold back. I will cry, too. This is not a time to be tough."

"But Daddy never cries."

"Yes, he did, dear. We soaked each other's shoulders many times, before and after you were born."

"Really?"

"Really. But you might want to cry quietly. Just let the tears flow and breathe normally. Do you think you can do that?"

Joe thought for a moment, then nodded solemnly. He reached out, gave his mother a hug, and stood back. He took a tissue from her dressing table and wiped his eyes.

"Where is everyone else?"

"Uncle Frank and Aunt Carrie are downstairs with *Grandmaman*. Grandpa went to the church. He'll be back before the limousine gets here. Then we'll all go together."

***

Meanwhile in Charlottesville, a dozen Army soldiers lined up to board the bus to Richmond. The driver thought they looked a little old, but they held themselves proudly. Each chest boasted no less than three rows of ribbons. A veteran himself, the driver recognized the Purple Heart on every man.

Without a word, they moved to the back of the bus, until the bus was three-quarters full of Negroes, with four empty rows up front.

***

Patrick O'Grady had been an usher at Saint Mary's ever since coming back from the war. It was comfortable. It was home. It was safe: from the Protestant kids who had bullied him in school, from the dark-skinned kids who lived in downtown Richmond, from a wide range of strangers and enemies. He had survived two years in Europe by shooting faster than anyone who moved, and the reflexes had never completely left him.

Coming up the street, Patrick saw a double column of men in uniform, marching toward the church. Most were Black, in Army and Marine uniforms. A Navy commander. A Marine general.

His first reaction was to move forward to bar the Negroes from the church. The general looked him squarely in the eye, as if daring him.

For the first time in his life, Patrick O'Grady backed down. He stood back, handing service bulletins to the men as they passed him. When they had filed into the church, Patrick stood in the door.

The military men filed to the right, down the side of the church, and filled in the pews. Patrick saw the officers take the last pew, except for the Navy commander, who sat in the next to last pew. There seemed to be no order to the others.

What the hell? he thought.

He waved at an altar boy lighting the candles, then sent him to the sacristy to get Father McMahon.

"What is it, Patrick?" asked the priest. The usher pointed to the right side of the church. The priest said, "Oh, yes. I'm sorry we didn't get the word out, but I only found out yesterday. Relax."

"But Father—"

"I said relax, Patrick. I've prayed for something like this for years. Too bad it has to be at Doctor Lockhart's funeral."

The priest patted him on the shoulder, then walked over to the last pew. He spoke a few words into the ear of the general, then returned to the sacristy.

Patrick saw the stretch limousine coming from the West End. The men from the funeral home were already at the curb, ready to open the doors. He only knew Nancy and little Joe, so he was surprised when an Army colonel and an elegant woman also got out of the car. The woman could only be Nancy's mother, the colonel her father. No wonder "little" Joe was already as tall as a third grader.

The other couple had to be Jason's brother and sister-in-law. The man was not an older version of Jason, but close enough.

The family went into the church, where they were met by more funeral home people and escorted to the front pews. The general exchanged a nod with Colonel Ardwood as they walked by.

As they passed the casket draped with an American flag, Joe reached up and ran his hand along its shiny surface. Then he kissed his hand the way he had seen pilgrims do in Europe two years before.

The last time his father had taken them on holiday, before he took ill.

The organist moved from background music to the prelude, an organ arrangement of the "Air" from the Orchestral Suite Number Three by J.S. Bach, familiar to most as *Air on a G-string*.

The congregation rose when the liturgical procession began from the back of the church. The sudden, single motion of three dozen men rising to attention caused many parishioners to glance to the right.

After a pause while the altar boys deployed to their positions, the priest began, "*Requiem aeternam dona eis…*"

Father McMahon's homily lasted less than five minutes, then he invited Frank Lockhart to deliver a eulogy. Frank broke down after two paragraphs, and looked through his tears at his wife, and then to the rows of soldiers, sailors, and Marines to his left.

"Please, sir," Frank choked, looking to the back of the church. The general was already standing. He moved to the lectern and embraced the grieving brother. While Frank went back to his pew, the officer turned to the lectern. A few gasps among the congregation signaled belated recognition.

He did not take out any notes. In a deep voice that carried easily to the back wall, he said,

"'Out of the deep have I called unto thee, O Lord: Lord, hear my voice.'

"We heard these words of the psalm a few minutes ago, and I have heard them more times than I want to remember." He paused, letting his words reverberate.

"But if there is any proof that God answers prayers, and that He does so through the hands of His servants, it is in this church today." He nodded to Matthew in the front row, then extended his hand to his left.

"Almost every man in uniform here was pulled from the brink by the man whose life we honor today. Hundreds more, in war and peace, owe their lives to Jason Joseph Lockhart, in North Africa, in Korea, in Equatorial Africa, and here in Richmond.

"And while his death leaves a hole in our lives, let us fill that hole with the love and devotion that he showed us in bringing us back from the deep."

With that, he turned sharply to the center of the stairs and returned to the rear pew.

Grief

NANCY LOCKHART BOLTED AWAKE. From Joe's room, a tiny voice screamed. "Noooo! Daddeee!" As she ran down the hall, she heard his sobs in between more screams.

"Wake up, Joe," she murmured into his ear, as she wrapped her arms around his shivering body. The sandy hair on the back of his head was wet in her hands. His pajamas were soaking hers.

Joe opened his eyes, recognized his mother, and buried his face in her chest.

After a minute or two, his shaking stopped. He backed up and looked into her eyes.

"It was Daddy again."

She hugged him, then held him away so they could talk.

"Want to tell me about it?"

"He was falling away, off a cliff. I think I pushed him." He dove into her chest again. "I'm sorry, Mommy, I didn't mean to." He began to sob again.

She squeezed him, then shook him gently.

"Joe! Listen!"

He leaned back, his tear-filled hazel eyes looking up at her. She thought. *Oh, God, why did he have to have*

Jason's hair and eyes? She forced herself to ignore the dagger in her own heart.

"Do you remember where Daddy was when he died?"

"Hospital."

"Yes. Can you tell a nightmare from the real world?"

He stared at her, thinking hard for a moment.

"I think so."

"Good. This was a nightmare, a bad dream. It can't hurt you, and it isn't true. You did not push your Daddy, did you?"

The pause made her uncomfortable, until he shook his head.

"I didn't think so." She kissed his head. "Let's get you some dry pajamas." She pulled back the blankets, then pointed to the dresser. He got out and chose a fresh set. His hair was already almost dry.

When he had put on his pajamas, he sat on the edge of the bed. She sat next to him.

"It felt so real. Why?"

"It's part of what we go through when someone we love leaves us. You love your Daddy, don't you?"

He nodded solemnly. "Do you have nightmares, too?"

"Yes, dear. So far, I have woken up before you did, or you would have heard me screaming, too."

He looked at her for a while, then his expression turned serious.

"Do you dream of pushing Daddy off a cliff?"

Nancy suppressed the memory of cocktail parties where adults joked about doing just that to their spouses. *Had Joe been eavesdropping?*

"No, dear, but I do imagine other terrible things happening. Over and over. Then I wake up crying or sweaty, just like you."

He put his arms around her. *My God, he can reach around me already!*

"Can I come if I hear you having a nightmare?"

She thought a while.

"Yes, dear. That would be helpful, I think. Just touch me and call my name. If I'm moving around, stand back. I might hit you before I wake up. Can you do that?"

He nodded again. "I can do that."

"Good. We'll see each other through this, okay?"

"Okay." He pulled up and kissed her on the cheek. Then he swung into bed and let her tuck him in.

"You can go to sleep, Mommy. I'm okay now."

***

Triage in the emergency room. Nancy struggled to quickly assess one broken body after another and point as the ambulances lined up outside the automatic doors. Their sirens winding down added to the general din of relatives beginning to gather outside the ER. She pointed in one of three directions, so that the orderlies could wheel the wounded or the dead to the appropriate level of care.

What am I doing here? I'm a clinical researcher, not an ER surgeon! Jason was the surgeon. She hadn't wielded a scalpel since World War II.

The next gurney rolled up. She looked down into the bleeding face of her husband, lover and tennis partner.

"Jason!" The gurney vanished, and the next one rolled up. Jason's face looked up at her again.

She screamed.

"Mommy! Wake up!"

She felt a small hand take the scalpel from her hand and hold it. The room whirled around her, went black, then resolved into a dark bedroom.

Her eyes followed the hand holding hers. The little head was even with hers.

"Joe."

"Nightmare, Mommy?"

She swung out and sat on the edge of the bed, putting out her arms. He jumped in her lap, knocking the breath out of her before she wrapped her arms around him and held on tight.

"Yes, dear." She held him quietly, while her heart settled down.

"Do you want to tell me about it?"

She almost laughed at his serious expression.

"Why not? You told me yours. Remember what triage is?"

"Daddy said it was sorting the wounded so he could patch up the worst cases first. He did that in the war."

"Very good, Joe! I dreamed I was in the emergency room at Saint Mary's doing triage after some terrible event downtown. The ambulances were lining up bringing the wounded to us. But each person on the gurney was your father, one after another."

"That sounds terrible. What did you do?"

"I screamed at the second one. Then your hand reached in and pulled me out of the nightmare." She hugged him. "Thank you, Joe."

"You're welcome, Mommy. Anytime."

"That sounds so grown up. These dreams should slow down after a while. I sure hope so."

"Me, too."

"We're up now. Want some hot chocolate?"

Joe's little face broke into a big smile.

"Yes, please!"

Home from the sea, at last

IT'S A WONDER the tracks are not underwater more often, Mike thought. The New York Central train flew upstream under gray skies as raindrops streaked the windows. The swollen Hudson River seemed to be just below the windows, making it feel as if the river were higher than the rails.

As the train slowed for the station stop at Albany-Rensselaer, he remembered the last time he had passed this way. The remnants of a hurricane had dumped record-breaking amounts of water on the region, driving the Mohawk River and the Erie Canal over their banks, and forcing Margery and him to take shelter for three days in a bed-and-breakfast. *I've never seen the sun in Albany.* Still, they had enjoyed the ride down the Erie Canal as far as Schenectady. It had been a memorable holiday.

This trip carried more stress with it than just the weather. He had a ticket to Buffalo, New York, and another from there to Cleveland, Ohio. A cheap bicycle he picked up at a Salvation Army thrift store for cash hung in the baggage car. The people he would meet had no idea just when he would appear. Only one person knew where.

West of Utica, the train pushed through the front. He felt his heart lift a little as the deep gold of the setting sun reflected off the clouds behind him and the wet fields on either side. Just before midnight, he rolled the bike across the platform in Rochester and rode in the dark to the Naval Reserve Training Center west of the city.

***

"This way, Commander." The chief petty officer who met him at the back door of the building pointed to the parking garage behind the center. They walked to a blue van parked by the bike rack. Mike slipped the bicycle into the rack and tossed his backpack into the van.

"Can you make sure the bike goes to a local recycle bike shop?"

"No problem, sir. Got one up the block from my house. Someone in the neighborhood will be very happy."

"Thanks."

The chief put the van in gear and drove north to the village of Irondequoit. At the pier by the yacht harbor, a boat was idling. Like Mike, the crew wore civilian clothes, but the gray paint job made it look suspiciously like a naval vessel.

Six hours later, morning twilight was just breaking in the east as Commander L. Michael Norwood, US Navy, stepped onto a pier in Tommy Thompson Park in Toronto, Canada. A gray Toyota sedan was waiting. The park was closed, and the driver was the only person to see the American officer vanish.

***

Four thousand miles away, a Fiat 1500 with five Italians approached the border checkpoint between Fernetti, Italy, and Sezana, Yugoslavia. The car radio blared the latest hits from San Remo, and the young men sang in hearty harmony as the driver slowed. He waved his driver's license at the guard and pointed to the cluster of brilliantly lit gas stations two hundred meters away.

The guard waved them through, shaking his head at the carload of frivolous youths enjoying a Saturday night. For them, Yugoslavia was where you bought cheap fuel for your car. The guard could not dream of owning a car, much less putting fuel in it. But such things were far from his mind that night. His wife of three months was waiting for him at home, and he could not care about anything else tonight.

At the last station, the car pulled alongside the farthest pump, which was shaded from the neon lights. The men made a show of getting out and singing as they danced around the driver, who was fueling the car. He swatted them good-naturedly. Some of the men went to the restroom and returned.

Tank topped off and debt paid inside the store, the driver and his friends rolled out and returned to Italy in the dark. When they were gone, a man slipped out of the restroom and melted into the woods.

***

"*Da questa parte, professore.*" This way, professor. Mike gently led the older man down the rock-strewn path through the woods to the rocky beach hidden from the lights of both Trieste and Capodistria. The shallow water was just choppy enough to mask the rubber boat that should be arriving soon. Mike motioned for them to sit on some boulders under the trees at the edge of the beach.

Sharing a meal bar from his backpack with the other man, Mike pondered the feeling of déjà vu of this entire mission. More than twenty years ago, he had led a pair of downed pilots and two injured Italian partisans to this same spot after carefully dodging German patrols for a week. Then, he had been a young sergeant detailed to the Office of Strategic Services (OSS) for his backcountry skills and his knowledge of German and Italian. That he was young and strong helped.

Now he was wondering what his twilight tour would be before he retired from the Navy. The stretched scar tissue from the wound at Inchon made his chest and shoulder ache. He needed the stop as much as the other man, though he hid it as best he could.

This time, he shepherded an Italian scientist who had been captured by the Soviets at the end of World War II. Only about 160 cm tall, the man was so thin that Mike had lifted him over fallen trees and other obstacles as they trekked from the outskirts of Ljubljana to the coast. Many of the scientists interned in Germany during the war had escaped westward as the Third Reich crumbled, but this man had not gotten out before his laboratory was overrun.

The researchers on the Manhattan Project had never forgotten Ernesto Pirrone, but not until the Hungarian Revolution in 1956 could he get a message to them. A special NATO working group gathered an interagency team to extract him. It took years to set up this operation. Late in the planning, Commander Norwood had been the only one in the room who was familiar with the territory and possibly able to guide the scientist to safety without attracting attention.

"How long?" asked the scientist in Italian.

"Ten minutes. How are you doing?"

"Okay now. Coming down that cliff was scary."

"You did well, like an *alpino.*" A mountain soldier. They smiled at each other.

In the surf, Mike spied an interruption in the line of the waves.

"Here they come."

When the Zodiac was a few meters out, Mike and the scientist hurried to the water's edge. Mike lifted the man into the boat even before it touched the shore.

Rifle fire erupted from the trees, with shouts in Italian and Slovene. Mike felt his shoulder explode, then his vision imploded, and the stars above him disappeared.

***

Bright light came through his eyelids. He knew not to open his eyes suddenly. Instead, he turned his head and peeked through slits. A shadow blocked the light.

"Welcome back, commander." Mike opened his eyes. An Army nurse stood by the bed, leaning over to shade him from the overhead neon lamps. As she rubbed her stethoscope on her shirt, she took his arm and began reading his vital signs.

"Where am I and what happened?"

"Camp Ederle in Vicenza. You were shot in the left shoulder. The team that brought you here is waiting for you to wake up."

"How long?"

"Just three days." She stood back and made a note on his chart. "The sleep after surgery was good for you. I'll send someone in."

"Thank you, nurse."

Mike was surprised that he felt so good. The wounded shoulder only ached – until he tried to move it. Gingerly, he poured some water into the glass on his bed table. He was finishing it as a doctor entered the room.

"Commander Norwood. I'm Doctor Barnes."

"Mike. Can you tell me more about what happened during the mission?"

"Only enough to say that you and the other man were successfully evacuated. I'll let your people know. They're waiting in the lobby."

Five minutes later, two men in civilian suits and an Italian Army officer came in.

"Commander Norwood, I'm Red Hanson and this is Gerry Monroe. Colonel Vitale here commanded the reception team for Professor Pirrone."

"How is he?"

"Fine. Reunited with his family, although dismayed that his wife died while he was behind the Iron Curtain."

"Mission accomplished. That's good."

"Yes," said Vitale, "and the boat crew from the submarine send their thanks for stopping the bullet before it hit the Zodiac."

"Makes it worthwhile, then."

***

Coming out of the Customs area at McGuire Air Force Base, Mike saw Margery at the edge of the crowd of dependent spouses and children. His heart swelled as powerfully as it did the first time he saw her on Main Street in Annapolis. The wind had blown her cap off. It flew straight at him, and he caught it. They both had paused in a moment of amazement before she started toward him. He met her and returned the cap.

Every time he saw her when coming home, that scene replayed in his soul. They embraced and kissed, out of the way of the others. Someone sighed, and they disengaged.

"How did you know I would be here?"

"Navy wife network. You're not cleared."

"We need you in Special Operations."

"One of us is enough, dear. How's the shoulder?"

"Only hurts if I move it."

"Dirk said that this may be your last mission. That won't make me sad."

"I wasn't supposed to be going anywhere, but when we laid it out, I was the only logical choice to pull it off."

"Success?"

"Yes."

"Good." She knew not to ask for details. "It's four hours back, so we can have supper at home."

"Looking forward to it."

As she took the ramp back to Interstate 95 after lunch in Wilmington, Margery said, "Are you ready for a twilight tour yet?"

"Believe it or not, yes. I had a lot of time to think about it last week in the hospital."

"Have you made up your mind? Being in the zone for captain, you might be waiting for that."

"That's what I'm thinking. I don't know if this injury will affect my promotion."

"I take it the mission was impressive enough, or they would not have risked a senior commander on it."

"There's that. The board should be out next month. Then we'll know."

God, it feels good to be going home, he thought. *It's time to stay for a while.*

***

Margery picked up the phone in the hall. She came into the study, where Mike was unpacking his briefcase.

"It's Dirk." Dirk Masden had been Mike's executive officer in the destroyer that Mike had commanded before he was sent to Special Operations. Now Dirk was the secretary of the captain selection board. No one was supposed to know that, but Margery was LeeAnn Masden's best friend.

"Hello, Dirk."

"Captain Norwood, I'm glad you're back, sir."

"Dirk, I'm not your skipper anymore. You don't have to 'captain' me."

"The board just let out, Mike. I couldn't wait to let you know."

Mike forgot to speak for a while.

"Thanks, Dirk. Thanks very much."

"You're welcome. Just you and Margery for now, please. The results will come out over the weekend."

"Understood. Give my best to LeeAnn." He cradled the handset.

Margery came to him from the door to his study. "I already sent your blues to the tailor for re-striping. Congratulations, dear."

"You knew?"

"Not officially, but I was willing to bet on it, so I jumped in front of his other customers."

He embraced her. They shared a long kiss, then went to the living room for a glass of wine. Dinner was in the oven.

"I need to update my preference card. The detailer may give me something I don't want anymore."

"What have you been thinking about?"

"I don't want to make admiral. I think I want my last assignment to be someplace where we could live after I hang up the uniform."

"Any ideas?"

"Too many. There are only nine blocks on the preference card."

"I may be able to help. You have said often enough how much you like Charlottesville."

"Yes." Mike had visited the Miller Presidential Center often when doing the research for his PhD dissertation.

"And Storrs. And New Haven. And San Francisco."

"Have we been anywhere we did not like?"

"No, but guess what all those places have? As do Lawrence Kansas, Chicago Illinois, Ann Arbor Michigan, and New York City?"

Mike shrugged. "What?"

"NROTC Units." Naval Reserve Officer Training Corps. "And each one needs an academically qualified four-striper."

"How did you figure that out?" His surprise was obvious.

"I grew up with this. You're the dumb grunt who transferred in from the Army."

Mike laughed. Margery's father had been the Commandant of Midshipmen at the Naval Academy in Annapolis when they met. She had watched the inner workings of the Navy all her life.

"So, I ask for the NROTC Unit at the University of Virginia?"

"The incumbent retires in August. Placement should be getting a fill request soon."

"You are amazing. Simply amazing."

***

In August, Captain L. Michael Norwood assumed command of the NROTC Unit at UVA. The Government Department invited him to join the faculty as an associate professor, so he had a professional home after he hung up his uniform.

That summer, Margery helped him outline the research plan for his first publications. He would be eligible for tenure only two years after joining the department as a full-time civilian professor. He should have two books and several articles published by then.

They bought the house they were renting and put in a garden out back.

Home is the sailor, home from the sea…

Joe meets the Dama

JOE LOCKED HIS BICYCLE to the parking sign outside the Borghese Gallery. The trees that had inspired the first movement of Ottorino Respighi's *Pines of Rome* cast a welcome shadow over him as he caught his breath and let the breeze cool his sweat-soaked body.

The Villa Borghese, Rome's vast central park and botanical garden, was one of the few spaces in the Eternal City that allowed the wind to move without having the closely packed buildings and asphalt roads heat it up. Joe did not mind the workout. It was only a half hour from school to the Borghese Museum, and the long, smooth downhill runs to the Tiber River from either end made up for the climbs.

Today's excuse to come to his favorite museum was a homework assignment. Brother Matthew had assigned his students in the Introduction to Art History class to write a report on one of the sculptures in their textbook. Joe had quickly volunteered to research Bernini's *Apollo and Daphne*. He had recently read the story in Ovid's *Metamorphoses* in Latin class (a painful exercise comparing four different translations to the original Latin).

He spent some time in the room studying the sculpture from different angles. He tried to imagine just how fast the metamorphosis of Daphne into a laurel tree would take and whether Apollo would not have had time to grab her anyway. *It is, after all, a snapshot in marble.* He could see the movement of the transformation but could not know at what point the scene looked just like this.

Not wanting to lose the idea of the snapshot or a movie still, Joe went to the windowsill, where he could set his notebook. He wrote some thoughts about speeds and stills, then closed the notebook to consider the sculpture again.

He tried to picture a naiad like Daphne today. Then he got tickled thinking about how his mother, Nancy Lockhart, would have reacted to a stalking Apollo. Unlike the river god Peneus, Joe's grandfather would never get a call for help from his daughter. More likely, General Matthew Ardwood would be proud that his stubborn girl could take care of herself. *Probably deck Apollo with her championship backhand.* He chuckled at the image of a Greek god nursing a black eye on the ground after getting fresh with the former tennis pro.

The security guard scowled at him.

"*Scusi.*" Sorry. Joe was still grinning when he left the room. He wanted to write two reports on this assignment, one for Brother Matthew, the other for himself. If the monk seemed to be in a good mood, he might share both stories.

***

On his way back to the main entrance, he paused at the room that held Italian Renaissance paintings, specifically from the sixteenth century. A portrait of a girl in a red dress caught his eye. He remembered this picture from the plates in the center of his art history textbook. *Dama con Liocorno*. Lady with a Unicorn.

She is lovely, he thought. More than lovely, the blond woman, who could not have been any older than Joe, was beautiful. She looked out from the scene with a confidence and maturity that spoke of a life of power and daring deeds ahead of her. Usually, portraits of Renaissance brides looked their age, hardly ready for the altar or for the responsibility of running a noble household.

Joe admired the *Dama* for a few minutes, then left, resolved to look up more information on her.

***

The *Dama* was indeed Joe's age, but only in the memory of the artist, Raffaello Sanzio. Various experts disagreed as to whether the young noblewoman was Caterina Gonzaga, Giulia Farnese, or Maddalena Strozzi. All three families were household names in Italy. Joe read about them in Maria Bellonci's biography of Lucrezia Borgia, who was a fast friend of Giulia Farnese. Maddalena Strozzi was the bride of the wealthy art patron of Florence, Agnolo Doni. Doni had commissioned portraits of himself and his bride from Raffaello.

Caterina, Giulia, Lucrezia, and Lucrezia's sister-in-law, Isabella d'Este, were no more than two years apart. The first three were "natural" children, which Joe knew would be called "love children" today. Their fathers recognized them, so they benefited from being noblewomen, but they had a special perspective on the patriarchal world around them. Each of them spent years running their husbands' cities, including directing armies, surviving sieges, and cleverly escaping the Sack of Rome by Charles VI of France. The husbands were variously absent at war or useless.

Joe sided with the historians who argued that the bride in the picture was Caterina Gonzaga. In real life, she had even won a beauty contest of sorts against Giulia Farnese, in the report of which both women had been described in detail.

Brother Matthew was not happy the following Monday when Joe asked for an extension on his report. Over the weekend, he had lost himself in Bellonci's book, and the contradictory analyses of the *Dama con Liocorno*.

With some midnight oil on Monday night, he produced a report on the sculpture, combining information from the encyclopedia with his observations about Bernini's capturing the movement in a photographic moment. The teacher gave him a B for being late. Joe asked if he would look at a different report, in the form of an updated story. The cleric agreed to look at it when it was ready.

***

"Apollo, would you pull-eze stop moping at the window?" Leto never stopped stroking the razor edge of her sword with a whetstone. She huffed an impatient noise. "It's Daphne again, isn't it?"

"How do you know?" Apollo turned from the window and crossed his arms.

"I'm your mother. I always know." She smiled at her handsome—no, her beautiful—son. "Besides, your shoulders always sag a certain way when you think of her. You have different poses for the others."

Apollo shrugged. Leto tested the sword on a two-by-four, cutting it cleanly across. She sheathed the weapon.

"Much as I hate what Eros did to you, I must admit that it's a little ridiculous for you to go on like this. Give it up, son."

"I can't."

"You're a god, dummy. Of course, you can."

"What do you suggest?"

"You could apologize to Eros, or Cupid, or whatever they call him now."

"Humans pull out pictures of him to celebrate some guy named Valentine. Crazy mortals: Valentine was chargrilled, and they give each other chocolates in his honor."

"I never did understand what your father saw in them." Leto knew that Zeus had plenty of mortal lovers in addition to the goddesses he admitted to.

"You really think apologizing would do any good?"

"It couldn't hurt. He might have forgotten about it by now, and no one on Earth seems to care much what we do." She put a kettle on the range and arched an eyebrow at the god. He nodded and got out two mugs.

"Besides," Apollo said, "he may look like a silly boy, but he is almost three thousand years old and a damn good shot. Still, I've never apologized to anyone."

"Try it. What's the worst he can do?"

Apollo sat in the windowsill and thought. The cold air on his back made him jump back into the room. Living in the clouds above Mount Olympus was always chilly except on the hottest days.

"I'd expect him to refuse to accept the apology. He can really hold a grudge. But if he starts crowing about the apology, I think I'll lose my cool."

"What would you ask him to do? I mean, assuming he accepts the apology."

"I'd like to be free of this longing. After I got over the rage of Daphne escaping me, I thought I was in love, but I realized that I needed to let her go. I was just horny—don't say anything!" He grinned as she let her breath out. "Coronis and Kyrene helped me understand that. But you see the moping. I can't get over Daphne."

"Sounds like you still are in love. Tough for an immortal, you know."

"Tell me about it! I went looking for her, but the woods were gone. It's a suburban shopping mall now."

He went to the cabinet and got out the bowl of ambrosia paste. He scooped some into the mugs. Leto poured the hot water. They stirred the warm ambrosia in silence for a while.

"I have an idea. Take your sister with you."

"Artemis doesn't have anything to do with this."

"Maybe not. But she is a better shot than Eros, even if the 'silly boy' doesn't think so. You were always clever, and he's a sucker for a dare. Bet him that he can't outshoot her. When he loses, he can back out the curse of his golden-tipped arrows." She took a sip. "Do you know where she is?"

"Playing basketball with the girls at the high school." He tilted his head toward the sprawling metropolis of Athens. "She won't want to be bothered."

"Maybe not, but take her some fresh clothes and a towel. She always forgets them, and she always wants a shower or a bath after playing ball."

"Okay. Don't wait up for us for supper, then. I want to go to the Palomar Observatory tonight and look at Orion with her."

"Good move. That will help her understand how important this is to you."

"Thanks, Mom. You're the best." He kissed her on the cheek.

"Don't tell your stepmother. Now go on, before you have to chase her like one of her dogs."

***

Brother Matthew liked the story enough to raise Joe's mark to B+. He also suggested that Joe submit it to the *Roman Eagle*, the school newspaper.

"Thank you, Brother. May I ask if we are going to study all the plates in our book?"

"Probably not, Joe. We don't have time. But we will wrap up the Renaissance next week with another field report like this one. Are you anxious to write another story?"

"Maybe. I asked because I recognized the *Dama con Liocorno* in the Borghese when I went to study *Apollo and Daphne*. It's in our book."

"Do you want that one?"

Joe shrugged. "Sure."

"Good. I'll put you down for it. The others can pick something else tomorrow. Your reward for this story. I enjoyed it."

"Thanks, Brother."

The next week, Joe turned in his report. Raffaello, Caterina and her friends got him an A this time.

Years later, the *Dama* would enter Joe's life dramatically. But he would not get a grade for that story…

Lockhart Chapter 1: Bomb

JOE LOCKHART FELT and heard a thump ahead as he coasted downhill. A mass of hot September air rolled over him like a gust of wind. He sped past the traffic that choked downtown Rome during the lunch hour, even on the weekend. On his left stood the American Embassy, still called Palazzo Margherita by the locals. Wondering about the noise, he decided not to stop at the Embassy Annex to his right, where he had been going.

As he negotiated his way across the oncoming and left-turn traffic in front of the embassy, the smooth asphalt of the Via Veneto turned into the bone-jarring cobblestones of the Via Bissolati. Then he recognized the smell of burning oil.

He expected to see a stalled car with smoke pouring from its engine. But the traffic still moved past the international airline offices that lined both sides of the street. The sun reflected off the walls and windows of the tall buildings, aggravating the heat and the oppressive, oily feel of the smoke.

Traffic began to back up. The wail of sirens came up behind him. Pulling his bicycle over, he put a foot on the curb to watch two police cars and a fire truck go by. Beyond the bend, he could hear them stop.

Joe dismounted and pushed his bike onto the sidewalk. Ahead, the firemen hauled hoses across the street while the police funneled the bumper-to-bumper traffic into Via San Basilio and Via Carducci, on either end of the scene.

Black smoke billowed from a burning car and flames licked the front of the Pan American Airlines ticket office. The ground-floor windows gaped like monstrous mouths. Glass and debris lay everywhere. And two bodies.

A young woman leaned up against the building. Her body made an unnatural right-angle bend from the pavement up the wall, and her hand still clutched the shopping bag flattened against the wall. Joe's stomach quivered. The blackened corpse had no face.

The other body was only legs, sticking out of the window of the ticket office. The rest of him was inside. Fresh blood ran onto the sidewalk. Joe froze. He felt alone, looking from outside himself.

The firemen moved quickly to spray water and foam on the flames. Ambulances and more police cars arrived.

"*Dietro, ragazzo!*" Back, boy! A rough hand on his arm snapped Joe back to reality. A cordon of police shoved him and the gathering crowd back up the Via Bissolati. Mounting his bike, he pedaled into the stalled traffic, back toward the American Embassy.

His stomach gave him just enough warning to pull into the side street that went behind the embassy. He jumped off his bicycle and ducked under the overhang of the large fountain on the corner. There, he threw up and held on to the wall until the shivering stopped. The mess ran through a grate into the sewer below. Joe cleaned himself at the fountain and rinsed his mouth. After a long drink of cold water, he waited for his pulse to settle. Even on the hottest days, the greenery hanging over the wall of the embassy created a cool corner next to the fountain. The spring blooms had long since fallen, but the sweet fragrance of the plants soothed him.

Joe needed to return some books to the US Information Service library in the Embassy Annex and look for a book about Admiral Farragut for a history report. He rode back up the Via Veneto.

The annex occupied a seventeenth-century palazzo between two luxury hotels. The entrance hall had a *Stars & Stripes* newsstand and mini bookstore on the left, with the USIS library on the right. Directly ahead, a pair of swinging doors led into the lobby, with the Army Post Office service counter. Most of the offices inside were manned by armed forces personnel and civilians working for the Military Advisory Assistance Group, which oversaw the Marshall Plan. Though Italy had recovered from World War II, the massive organization that had rebuilt Western Europe in less than fifteen years was still winding down. Government agencies that normally did not operate overseas maintained liaison offices in the annex, such as the FBI, the Department of Agriculture, and the Coast Guard.

The cool air inside the doorway reminded him sharply how hot it was outside. As he was about to turn right, he noticed a young woman with her arms filled with newspapers and books trying to open the door from the *Stars & Stripes* shop. He turned and held the door for her.

"Thanks," she said, with a smile that reached her blue eyes. "I should remember to do this in different trips." Obviously American, with her blond hair in the bouffant style, she wore a light blue cotton blouse and a beige skirt. Joe walked over to the heavy, swinging doors to the lobby and held one for her.

"No problem. Have a nice day."

"You, too." She smiled again, then smoothly moved through the door toward the grand staircase on the left. *I've held countless doors for women*, he thought, *so why am I holding my breath?* With a silent sigh, he stepped down into the library.

The place was probably the size of a small-town library in the US. He wasn't sure about that, never having lived in a small town. Dark wooden shelves lined the circular room. Smaller, free-standing bookcases shared the floor with couches and reading desks. Daylight from the street came from long windows at ground level, which covered the upper half of one wall. Library patrons could see the waists and legs of the pedestrians on the broad sidewalk outside. The card catalog and the librarian's station formed a circular fortress of wood and marble in the center of the room.

He found what he was looking for and sat at one of the tables. The images and the smells of the car bombing made concentration impossible. He decided to check out the book and go home. Soon he was riding down the smooth, open roads that crossed the Villa Borghese gardens and coasting to the Piazzale Flaminio. What used to be the assembly point for triumphal marches by the Roman legions was now a vehicular madhouse. Buses from several different lines met the trolleys, and passengers ran between them. Romans hoped to have a subway station there someday. Joe took back streets to the Lungotevere delle Navi, then upstream to the Risorgimento Bridge over the Tiber River. A quick ride among the trees along the Viale Mazzini brought him to the foot of the Monte Mario overlooking the city, and the sweaty climb home.

***

"It would have been so much worse on a weekday," said Nancy Lockhart, reading about the bombing in the newspaper that evening. Sitting in a comfortable armchair in the living room, she wore a plaid skirt and a white cotton blouse. Only on Saturdays could she skip the business suit, hose, and heels. "The ticket offices were closed for lunch, too, so the usual crowds of airline travelers weren't there."

Joe looked up from the couch, where he was taking notes with a copy of *Damn the Torpedoes, Full Speed Ahead: The Story of Admiral David Farragut* on his lap. "Who did it?" he asked.

"They still don't know, but a neofascist group threatened something like this yesterday. Did you see this picture?" She turned the paper around to show him a photo on the front page. It was the woman with the shopping bag.

Joe nodded and turned back to his book. His mother did not need to know just how close he had gotten to the blast.

"Some of the people in the office are convinced that the right wing is planning a coup, but almost as many believe that it would be impossible." Nancy folded the newspaper. "Did you finish that history report?"

"Almost."

"You won't have time tomorrow if we want to go to Tivoli after church."

"Okay, Mom. I know. When do you want to eat?"

"Let's walk down to the piazza for supper. We both have too much work to do for cooking and dishes."

Their housekeeper-cook, Angela Ceccarelli, had stocked the small refrigerator for the weekend. Joe's mother was a good cook, but she and Joe also enjoyed these walks to the tree-lined Piazzale delle Medaglie D'Oro at the top of the Monte Mario. Sometimes they would walk to the Parco della Vittoria near the *piazzale*, with its stunning view of the Eternal City. Nancy Lockhart was tall for a woman, with the grace and form of the champion tennis player that she had been. She had rich, auburn hair, while his was sandy colored like his father's. Joe was taller than she. With bright hazel eyes, long lashes, and a similar nose and mouth, people often mistook them for siblings, rather than mother and son.

It was dark by the time they reached their favorite *rosticceria*. Pointing to the food under the display window, Nancy picked the roast chicken with roast potatoes; Joe asked for sliced *porchetta*, the traditional Roman roast pork with rosemary and other herbs, also with potatoes. They took their trays to one of the Formica-topped tables in the brightly lit room. Back home less than an hour later, Nancy went into her study to work. Joe sat at the dining room table, finishing up the history report.

***

That night, Joe dreamed about the bomb, but the body in his dream was that of his father. Screaming penetrated his sleep. The smoke from the burning car cleared. He found himself looking up at his mother's terrified face. She was shaking him.

"My God, Joe!" She let go when she saw he was awake. "What was it? You haven't screamed like that since you were nine."

At first, he could not answer. Sweat had soaked his bed linens and pajamas, and he began shivering. Nancy hugged her son, dampening her own nightgown. The only light came from the street. Brakes squealed; someone was making the turn to go down the hill.

"It was Dad." He stopped shaking. As he swung out of bed, she pulled the covers off. "Already I can't remember the surroundings much, but he had no face." He went to the dresser for some fresh pajamas. "I think I'll be okay now, Mom."

Nancy went to the linen closet for some sheets. "Are you sure? I will never forget the nightmares when you were little. They went on for two years after your father died."

"This feels different," Joe said. "This scene was like the picture of the bomb in the paper."

They remade the bed together in silence.

"Want some hot chocolate?" she asked when they had put the wet sheets in the laundry hamper.

"That would be good." Joe slipped into dry pajamas, then followed his mother to the kitchen. She had put a kettle of water on. When she turned around, he saw the tears running down her face.

"Mom, what's wrong?" He crossed the room and hugged her.

"Nothing really, except the feeling." She let herself sob against her son's shoulder. "Doctor Lambert told us that these dreams would come back every so often. I wasn't ready. It's been almost ten years. All the pain of watching you scream came back to me. God, it was terrible. You were so helpless."

Joe fought back the lump in his throat.

"Wasn't he the one who gave me Tootsie Rolls?"

"Yes, and you always left the sticky things in the car." She laughed despite the tears.

"He never figured out that I didn't like them." He chuckled, grateful for the distraction.

The kettle whistled. Joe went to the stove with the cocoa while Nancy got out the cups. She found some cookies and set them out.

They sat across from each other at the kitchen table. The hot chocolate felt good.

"Mom, did Doctor Lambert say how long this would last?"

"He said that we would carry your father's death with us for the rest of our lives. Most of my colleagues said he was wrong to let you into the hospital so much near the end. But I had a hunch he was right."

"I don't like remembering Dad that way, but I wouldn't have wanted to stay home. I know he wanted me there." He tried to picture his father as the strong, handsome man he had been, not the shriveled skeleton he became, wasting away in the Saint Mary's hospital in Richmond, Virginia.

"Nights like this, I'm not so sure," she said.

"I'll be okay, Mom. I'm not nine anymore. The details are fuzzy, but it didn't feel like the old dreams. It was something else."

She reached across and squeezed his hand.

"Look at this. You wake up screaming, and I'm the one getting help."

"It's your line: 'we're a team now.'"

Back in bed, Joe realized that his mother had not looked for her cigarettes the whole time they were up.

***

Six thousand miles away, Siegfried Kanter stubbed out his cigarette in the marble ashtray on the table. His company's security people had swept the suite in the Waldorf-Astoria, or he would not be having this conversation.

"Does anyone have a better idea?" His expression was severe, but then, it usually was.

"Not me, Sig." This from the Texan with his booted feet stretched beneath the coffee table. His sunburned face set off his white hair dramatically. The tallest man in the room, his lanky frame and the bolo tie betrayed his origins in the oilfields.

Beside him, the smartly dressed Italian shrugged. "I think it will work, gentlemen. As long as our pigeon does not wise up." He held himself erect, as befitted a recently retired general of the Italian Carabinieri Corps. "Do you think this channel will be secure, Sandro?"

A slightly plump man, Sandro was the only one of the four whose hair was thinning. Like them, he wore a custom-tailored suit and shoes. "It should work just fine, Ettore. The people in my office here have worked with him for years. He understands no Italian, so he won't understand anything not in English in the files he forwards to New York." He played with the Montblanc pen that his wife had given him.

"Our contacts in the Smithson Italia offices in Milano and Torino are ready to insert the codes into the company correspondence for New York before it goes to Rome," said the general. "Only the New York copies will have the coded information, so the others in Rome won't be suspicious."

Silence reigned as Siegfried looked around again. "Manfredo?"

"Nothing to say, really," said the fifth man in a British public-school accent. "I can't think of a better way to do this, in spite of my misgivings."

"Are we all agreed, then?" The other men nodded. "By next week, our companies will buy a minimum number of shares of Smithson Pharmaceuticals on the New York Stock Exchange to qualify for 'major investor' status. Any problems with that?"

"Are the carabinieri buying stock, too?" said the Texan with a grin. The others smiled. They knew that Ettore Arcibaldo was the only one likely to be exposed if the operation failed. The general's smile did not extend to his eyes.

Sandro raised his hand. "One thought. We should not all buy at once. I must move money from the home office in Zurich anyway. It would be less conspicuous if we made our purchases over two weeks."

"Makes sense," said the Texan. "Let me go first, then Sig early next week. Manny's a major investor, so if Sandro picks up his shares, say, one week after Sig, no one should notice."

"It will raise Smithson's share price," said Sandro, "but not enough to attract the attention of the financial press."

"Hey, we might cover our costs with this!" The Texan laughed at his own joke.

"That settles it, then." Siegfried turned to Arcibaldo. "Good luck, General."

They rose and shook hands. By prior agreement, they left the suite two minutes apart and did not gather for dinner. On Monday morning, each was back in his office, having gone to New York for a "shopping trip over the weekend." The general was in a public meeting in Rome with his political supporters.

***

That same evening, Officer Sean O'Toole stopped at the corner outside the United Nations building and turned back. The black Ford Fairlane with diplomatic plates had been parked in that spot all day yesterday. He shone his flashlight inside, but the car was empty and clean. He keyed his radio.

"3255 here. There's a car parked in front of the UN in the no-parking zone since yesterday. Diplomatic plates, but at roll call, we were briefed to be extra careful."

"No one at the UN works those hours," said the dispatcher. "Secret Service should know. Hang around, 3255."

"Ten-four."

O'Toole paced next to the car. The heat from the day was radiating back from the asphalt and concrete, making him sweat. He hoped that he could clock off on time tonight.

Ten minutes later, a black sedan pulled up behind the Ford. A tall man in a business suit got out and approached O'Toole, holding out his credentials. US Secret Service.

"Ashford, Diplomatic Protection Detail. What's with this car?"

"Been here since yesterday morning. Normally we'd ignore it because of the plates, but, you know, with tomorrow's show."

Ashford nodded as he returned to his car. He pulled out the microphone to his radio and called in the plate number to his office. In less than two minutes, he had his answer and waved to O'Toole.

"Stolen plates. Have the precinct get a tow truck here ASAP. And keep civilians away."

***

Manny Romero drove his tow truck into the NYPD impound lot with a wave to the guard at the gate. With the smooth confidence of years of practice, he turned into the last place at the end of a row, lining the Ford Fairlane up with the other cars. He lowered the sedan and unhitched it. After parking his truck in the garage, he walked home.

Special Agent Ashford reported the suspicious car to the FBI and sent a request to ATF (Alcohol, Tobacco, and Firearms Division) to have the car checked as soon as possible. Then he closed his office and went home to try to get some sleep before meeting the Italian delegation coming from Rome.

At ten a.m. the next morning, the President of Italy arrived at the United Nations with an escorted motorcade, the third of a dozen European leaders who would arrive that day.

Also, at ten a.m., the New York Fire Department responded to a call from the NYPD impound lot. The explosion at the end of a row of cars destroyed five vehicles and blew a hole in the fence. Flying pieces of fencing injured three bystanders outside. The newspapers carried the story on page six the next day. Their front pages carried pictures of heads of state arriving for the General Assembly of the United Nations.

Author's Notes

These stories first appeared on my blogs between 2014 and 2023.

Here are my notes concerning individual tales.

"Inchon" – The real *USS-973* did land at Red Beach during the Battle of Inchon. A mortar round injured three sailors. She operated off Korea as described in the story and served in the French Navy as *RFS Golo* from 1951 until 1959. I chose to set my story in real ships because I could not make up heroism such as the men and women at Inchon and in *USS Haven* (AH-12) showed in real life. The landing ship squadron really did coordinate a massive evacuation of non-combatants before the amphibious assault. The Chief Staff Officer of the squadron admitted that organizing that evacuation was the proudest achievement of his career, notwithstanding his many decorations for other things. The rest of the story, and especially the people, is my own creation. There is no resemblance between the fictional Mike Norwood and the last American CO of *USS-973*, Lt. Robert I. Trapp.

"<u>Jason's Last Wish</u>" – You may have wondered what caused Jason Lockhart's sudden death. The human immunodeficiency virus (HIV) was beginning to spread long before acquired immunological deficiency syndrome (AIDS) was identified in 1981.

"<u>Last Respects</u>" – To my knowledge, General Lewis B. "Chesty" Puller never attended the funeral of my character or uttered the words I gave him in this story, but I like to think he would have. In war and in peace, medical personnel are front-line heroes.

I hope you have enjoyed reading these stories as much as I enjoyed writing them. If so, do check out the series of novels that follow them. There are links to them on my website.

Any writer worth the name is grateful for the criticism of careful readers. Write to jt@jthine.com.

My thanks in advance.

JT Hine

Made in the USA
Middletown, DE
08 February 2025